V

D0892805

SUNLIT SUSPICION

The Spanish sun is supposed to heal Helen's heartbreak and prepare her for a new life. Instead, danger and intrigue disrupt the calm routine of her working holiday. Is the stranger in the downstairs apartment a criminal or is he an innocent under threat? Just when she thinks she has found a new love, well intentioned meddling brings the past back to haunt her and her future is thrown into turmoil.

SHEILA HOLROYD

SUNLIT SUSPICION

Complete and Unabridged

LINFORD
Leicester

First published in Great Britain in 2008

First Linford Edition
published 2009

British Library CIP Data

Holroyd, Sheila.
  Sunlit suspicion- -(Linford romance library)
  1. Romantic suspense novels.
  2. Large type books.
  I. Title II. Series
  823.9'2–dc22

  ISBN 978–1–84782–793–7

Published by
F. A. Thorpe (Publishing)
Anstey, Leicestershire

Set by Words & Graphics Ltd.
Anstey, Leicestershire
Printed and bound in Great Britain by
T. J. International Ltd., Padstow, Cornwall

This book is printed on acid-free paper

1

Outside, the warm Spanish sun lit up the calm blue sea and the sun worshippers were stretched out happily on the beach. Inside, Helen found it uncomfortably warm as she scrubbed the tiled floor and made sure the bathroom was spotless. Mary's call summoning her to lunch came as a definite relief and she climbed the outside staircase to where Mary was holding the door open while trying to make sure that neither of the twins escaped through it.

'Have you finished?' she asked anxiously, and sighed when Helen shook her head. 'I'm sorry it has been such a hard job this time. I will never let that Simmonds family near the apartment again. I don't know how they managed to get it so dirty.'

'It really wasn't that bad. I've just got

to finish the kitchen,' Helen assured her, while privately reflecting that Mary couldn't be choosy about who she rented the downstairs apartment to. She needed the money.

Mary's happy marriage had ended suddenly when her husband had been killed in a road accident. A year later, eager to make a new start, she had used the insurance money as a down payment on this building in the Spanish seaside resort of Sitges, south of Barcelona. It consisted of two generous apartments, one upstairs and one down, and her plan was to live upstairs and let the downstairs apartment to holidaymakers. With luck the income would cover the mortgage and leave her enough to live on till the three-year-old twins, Peter and Shula, were old enough to go to school, when she intended to get a job. Unfortunately she had moved in June, missing much of the summer season, and money was getting tight.

Lunch, as usual, was a light salad

followed by fresh melon, after which the twins consented to a short rest in their bedroom while Mary and Helen took their coffee out on the balcony that overlooked the sea.

'We'll see what the new lot are like when they arrive this evening. How many are coming?' Helen enquired.

Mary's brow wrinkled.

'I don't know. A Mr John Bridges contacted the letting agency and paid for a month. They told him it would sleep six, but he didn't say how many would actually be here. It could be a family, a group of friends or even a honeymoon couple who like space.'

Helen sipped her coffee and shrugged.

'Well, it's ready for them, however many come, and the weather is marvellous, so whoever arrives is sure to love it.'

Mary still looked unhappy.

'I hope so. The agent said people nowadays expect a private swimming pool, but I can't afford to put one in yet.'

Helen, as often happened, found herself reassuring Mary.

'We are two minutes' walk from the sea and a gorgeous beach. What more can they want? Now, finish your coffee and relax for a bit.'

When the twins woke up Mary decided she would take them shopping while Helen cleaned the downstairs kitchen.

'You'll be all right,' she told Helen. 'I'll be back before Mr Bridges and his party arrive. You can have a bit of peace and quiet.'

Helen followed her down the stairs, eager to finish her cleaning, and was on her knees in the kitchen checking the cupboards when suddenly her work was interrupted by a sharp knock on the door and she heard voices outside. Peering through the window, Helen saw a taxi parked in front of the house with the driver unloading suitcases and piling them on the pavement. The new tenant and his friends must have arrived early!

Someone was still knocking insistently on the apartment door so she grabbed the keys and hurried to open it, only to see a man retreating to the taxi.

'It's all right! I'm here!' she called out to his back.

He swung round and looked at her impatiently, and she became painfully conscious of her tousled hair and crumpled sundress.

'Are you John Bridges?' she asked, forcing a welcoming smile and hoping Mary would appear.

He nodded curtly.

'Welcome to Sitges! I'm Helen Corby. I'm afraid Mrs Picton had to go out, but I've got the keys here so I can let you in and show you round.' She peered into the taxi and was surprised to see it empty. 'Is the rest of the party coming separately?'

'There is no party. I shall be here by myself.'

She stared at him and he picked up a briefcase impatiently.

'Can we go in? I've had a long journey and I need a rest.'

As the taxi driver drove away, Helen hastily held open the door of the apartment while John Bridges put his briefcase inside. She began to rescue his suitcases from the pavement but he brushed her aside and picked them up himself and took them indoors.

Helen followed him and began to indicate the various rooms but he stopped her.

'I can tell the difference between a bedroom and a bathroom. What else have you got to tell me?'

She pointed out the toiletries in the bathroom and the box of basic supplies in the kitchen, indicated a folder on one of the worktops and opened it to pick up a map.

'This folder gives you all the information about the apartment and this map shows you the nearest shops and some restaurants we recommend.' She hesitated. 'Have you any questions?'

'None I can think of at the moment.'

'Mrs Picton will come to introduce herself as soon as she returns.'

'Ask her to leave that till tomorrow. I am really very tired.'

She looked at him uncertainly. He was tall and slim, probably in his mid-thirties, though the lines of fatigue she could see etched on his face made him look older. He was neatly dressed in a business suit and was even wearing a tie. He certainly didn't look like a man on holiday!

'I'll leave you then.'

He stood silent, obviously waiting for her to go, and she turned towards the door feeling like a schoolchild dismissed by a head teacher. Then she came back hastily.

'Oh, I nearly forgot. I was finishing the kitchen floor when you arrived. I'll just get my bucket.'

She prided herself on being calm and competent, but this man was making her feel flustered.

He was holding the door open for

her, more out of impatience than politeness, she decided.

'Here are your keys. Remember, if you want anything just come up the stairs and knock.'

Mary and the twins returned to find Helen feeling definitely disgruntled.

'I don't like him at all,' was her verdict on the new tenant. 'He was almost rude to me.'

Mary looked worried.

'Why would a man on his own want to rent an apartment for six? Perhaps he was coming with someone else and there was an emergency and they couldn't come. At least he paid in advance.'

'I can't imagine anybody wanting to come on holiday with him,' Helen snapped, still feeling very annoyed.

'Perhaps he'll improve when he has had a good sleep,' Mary said hopefully. 'I'm sorry you had to deal with him. In fact I'm feeling very guilty about you, Helen. I promised you a holiday by the sea and all you've done is clean, shop and look after the twins.'

Helen shook her blonde hair.

'That's not how I understood the agreement. You said you would give me free board and lodging in return for help with the apartments and the twins, and in my spare time I could see Spain.'

'Except that there has been very little spare time,' Mary sighed.

'I am enjoying myself,' Helen told her firmly, though to herself she admitted that the 'holiday' was proving rather tiring. Still, what else could she have been doing? As Helen drew near the end of her degree course in English Literature she had realised that few businesses wanted to employ someone whose main qualification was a knowledge of Milton and Elizabethan dramatists, and that she needed more saleable skills.

In late September she would start a teacher-training course, but meanwhile she had had no money for the summer holiday she felt she needed and she had welcomed eagerly her friend's invitation to come to Spain. Helen had worked through all her vacations to pay her way at university, aware that her family could not afford to help her, and this had been her first opportunity to come abroad.

In addition, there had been personal reasons why she wanted to get away from England for a while. On the whole she did not regret her decision. She and Mary had been friends from their schooldays and got on well together and there had, after all, been time to explore Sitges, a lovely town with many souvenirs of the days when it had been a favourite summer resort for artists from nearby Barcelona. Helen only wished she had had an opportunity to see Barcelona itself.

At eleven o'clock the next morning Mary went to meet her new tenant, taking the twins with her as potential icebreakers. She was back in ten minutes, red spots of anger glowing on her cheeks.

'You were right, Helen! He is a horrible man! He didn't even ask me in

— just stood there and didn't say a word more than was necessary. He made it clear he couldn't wait for me to go. I asked him if he would like to come up for coffee and he said, 'No'. Nothing else. Then I introduced the twins and he glared and said, 'I suppose they were making the thumping noises above me this morning. He's paid for a month, and if I didn't need the money I would give it back to him and tell him to go somewhere else.'

'Well, at least he's not going to take up much of our time,' Helen consoled her. 'Let's take the twins to the beach and forget about him.'

Sitges' curving golden beach, dominated by a church standing on a small headland, was an ideal playground for the twins. They scampered in and out of the water's edge and built sand-castles with enthusiasm. When this started to bore them, they involved Helen in a game where, basically, one of them threw a rubber ball as far as it would go and then they laughed at her as she ran after it.

One particularly good throw by Peter landed the ball in the sea. Helen hovered on the edge of the water, wondering whether to venture to the ball's rescue and risk getting her skirt wet or hope it would drift in within reach. As she reluctantly dipped one toe in the foam, a voice said, 'Allow me,' and a figure strode confidently past her, splashed its way to the ball, and emerged with it safely held in a large hand.

'Thank you,' Helen said gratefully. She considered the ball's rescuer. He was about thirty, stockily built, dressed in cut-off jeans and T-shirt, with a broad grin on a face that was pleasant, though not handsome. Her gazed became fixed, and he shrugged resignedly.

'Go on. Say it.'

'Say what?'

'That you've never seen anyone with such red hair.'

She could feel herself blushing.

'Well, it is very bright.'

It was a burning, glowing beacon.

At that moment the twins appeared on each side of Helen, curious about her new acquaintance. The man crouched down level with the children and held out the ball.

'Here! I guess this is yours.'

Peter seized the ball and he and his sister ran away, giggling.

'A lively pair. Are they yours?' said the stranger, looking after them.

'No,' Helen said, with a little more haste than was necessary. 'They belong to my friend, Mary.' She gestured vaguely to where Mary sat watching them. 'They live in Sitges, but I'm just here for a holiday. I'm Helen Corby.'

'I'm Harry Lyne. Like your friend, I live here. Do you like Sitges?'

'I love what I've seen of it.'

Mary was gathering up their possessions and waving to attract the twins' attention. It was time to go back for lunch before the children's nap. Helen started to move away.

'Wait!' Harry Lyne said. 'Have you

heard about the Sitges custom of taking a walk along the promenade when it's starting to get dark? We might see each other there one evening.'

It was not quite an invitation, but it would make a change from putting the twins to bed and then sitting in front of Spanish television, Helen thought, although Mary might not like to be left by herself.

'It was just a suggestion,' Harry Lyne said awkwardly, but cheered up as she smiled at him. 'I may see you sometime, then? I am usually near the church about seven o'clock.'

'You will be easy to find if I do come. I'll look for your red hair.'

Helen hurried after Mary, leaving him grinning.

'Who was that?' Mary enquired as they shepherded the twins home.

'He's called Harry Lyne, he lives in Sitges, and he practically invited me to meet him one evening.'

'That sounds a good idea. A date with a young man would be a change

14

from the widow and orphans.'

Helen shot a sidelong glance at her friend. Mary had loved her husband deeply, but she was still only twenty-five. She could not be expected to spend the rest of her life looking back at her happy past.

'Come with me. Maybe he's got a friend.'

'Maybe he has, but I haven't got a babysitter. No, you go out and enjoy yourself and then tell me all about it.'

With the twins fed and put to bed, the two friends once again began to speculate about the mysterious Mr Bridges. They hung over the balcony, peering downwards.

'The windows are all closed,' Mary pointed out. 'And there aren't any towels out to dry, so he can't have been swimming.'

'Whatever he's up to, the welcome food pack will soon run out and then he'll have to go shopping. Anyway, we provide cleaning services every other day, so I'll go down tomorrow to tidy up and that may give us an idea what he is doing with himself.'

The rest of the evening passed in pleasant idleness. As darkness fell Mary looked at Helen mischievously and asked her if she was going for a walk along the promenade. Helen laughed and shook her head.

'Certainly not! I don't want Harry Lyne to think I'm desperate to meet him again so soon. Anyway, it's time you had another computer lesson.'

Like many such firms, the agency which dealt with letting Mary's apartment conducted most of its business via the Internet. Mary had remained happily ignorant of computers until this fact forced her to use one. Helen, who prided herself on being computer-literate, had been introducing her to its many uses, from simply contacting the agency to keeping track of her finances, as well as setting up form letters for her to print and send to clients. Mary sighed resignedly.

'All right — provided I'm allowed to

play Solitaire on it for ten minutes after the lesson.'

The first thing Mary had to do was to check her emails to see if there was any news about clients, and she was pleased to learn that a family of five had booked a fortnight at the end of the season.

'I'm glad about that. I was told that was a difficult slot to fill. Oh!' She was gazing at the screen. 'And my parents are coming in a fortnight's time. It's Mother's birthday and she wants to spend it with us.'

'That will be nice,' Helen said in a carefully emotionless tone. Mary was looking apprehensive.

One of the reasons Mary had decided to settle in Spain was because her parents had already retired there. They lived south of Salou, further down the coast, and had expected Mary to come and live near them, but Mary had explained that not only was Sitges an attractive resort in its own right, but its nearness to Barcelona made it very appealing for people looking for holiday accommodation.

The other reason, as Helen well knew, was that it put a safe distance between Mary and her loving but over-possessive mother. After the freedom of married life, Mary did not want to return to being treated like a teenage daughter and having her life organised for her.

Before going to bed that night, Helen opened the window of the miniscule bedroom she occupied and stood gazing out at the starlit sky. Her stay here was a pleasant interlude before she returned to England, real work, and facing up to the past, and anyone she met here would soon have to be forgotten. Still, it might be pleasant to stroll along the promenade one evening with Harry Lyne when the heat of the day was past and the stars were shining overhead as brightly as they were tonight. A little masculine admiration would be very welcome after her encounter with Mr Bridges.

She saw a light shining on the lawn that surrounded the house, and by craning her neck she could see that the windows of the main room in the downstairs apartment were still lit up. She wondered idly what John Bridges was doing by himself, and whether the beauties of Sitges would be wasted on him.

2

About ten o'clock the following morning Helen heard the downstairs front door close and she saw John Bridges walking swiftly away in the direction of the shops. At least he had abandoned his suit in favour of jeans and a T-shirt.

'I wish he was a little more friendly,' Mary complained. 'Then we could have told him which are the best stalls in the market and things like that.'

'If he comes back with stale fish and limp lettuce that will be his own fault,' Helen said firmly. 'Anyway, while he's out I'll pop down and clean up the place.'

The rented apartment seemed almost as she had left it. There was a razor and a toiletries bag in the bathroom but that was almost the only sign of a tenant. The bed had been made and there was no dirty crockery. There were no books or magazines and the television had not even been plugged in. Maybe he passed the hours sleeping or meditating.

She shook out the mop and started on the living area, and as she mopped under the couch she felt something in the way. Bending down, she pulled out a slim laptop computer. Why had he brought that on holiday? Either he spent hours cruising the Internet or he was a computer games addict.

'What are you doing?'

The question came as a shout, immediately behind her. Helen jumped, nearly dropped the laptop, and clutched it to her. John Bridges let the carrier full of shopping fall on the floor and seized the computer from her. He looked furious.

'Why are you sneaking round here while I'm out? What were you doing with my computer?'

Helen felt her cheeks growing red with anger.

'I'm here to clean,' she told him sharply. 'You get maid service. It says so in the folder I gave you. You've made it clear that you don't like company so I thought it would be more convenient for both of us if I cleaned while you were out. As for the computer, look!' She pointed to the abandoned mop. 'How could I clean the floor without moving it from under the couch?'

'I see.' He still looked deeply suspicious. 'Well, in future I shall be grateful if you will knock and ask if it is convenient for you to come in and clean. I don't want you here when I'm out.'

'I'll tell Mrs Picton,' Helen informed him through clenched teeth. Deciding that she was not going to stay there with him to finish the floor, she picked up the mop and bucket and stalked out back to Mary's apartment, where her friend listened to her tale of woe in surprise and then spent some time soothing her.

'The man's an idiot!' Helen proclaimed.

'He certainly is! Unless . . . ' Mary

paused thoughtfully. 'Unless he has a good reason for wanting to make sure nobody knows what he is doing. Perhaps it's something illegal.'

Helen was taken aback. Rudeness was one thing, criminality another.

'How could it be?'

'Well, we're near Barcelona, and a big port always has a fair number of criminals. Maybe it is something to do with drug smuggling. There is a lot of heroin brought into Spain. Maybe he sits there, using his computer to contact smugglers and buyers. Maybe he's a Mr Big!'

Helen fidgeted.

'I think you are getting a bit carried away. Maybe he's just anti-social because he'd planned a romantic holiday with his girlfriend and then she dumped him. I can certainly under-stand why if she did!'

'Then why was he so worried about his computer?'

'Well, I have met people who do hate it when someone else even touches their computer. It has a lot of private information about them, remember.'

'Exactly. It might be private information that the police would like to know about.'

'Mary, we can't go to the police and say he made a fuss because I picked up his computer!'

Forced to agree, Mary sighed deeply. 'Oh well, next time you go down there, just see if you can find anything suspicious.'

'If he sees me poking and prying around he'll throw me out physically! Anyway, I was hoping you might do the cleaning next time. I don't want to see him again.'

'You know I'd have to take the twins with me. They love seeing what the tenants are like and they've got very friendly with some families, but I don't think Mr Bridges would welcome them, whether he's a drug smuggler or not.'

Helen could not argue with this. The rest of the day was filled as usual with housework, shopping and playing with the twins. As evening approached, Helen asked Mary if she would mind being left on her own for a couple of hours.

'Oh! I take it you are going to meet Mr Lyne?'

'I don't know. I'd like to walk along the promenade, but I won't be disappointed if I don't see him.'

At least it was true that Harry Lyne was not the only reason she looked forward to the evening. It was enjoyable to shed her usual jeans and T-shirt and carefully apply make-up after putting on a pretty dress. She brushed her hair and then stood back and admired her appearance, twirling round so that her skirt belled out.

'Pretty!' Shula's voice said approvingly, and she saw the twins standing in the doorway, solemnly observing her, so she kissed them both and led them back to their mother who was waiting to read them a story.

'Why can't Helen tell us a story?' Shula complained. 'I like her stories.'

'I'll tell you one tomorrow,' Helen promised. 'All about Princess Shula — and Prince Peter,' she added hastily as the little boy's face darkened.

She gave a final glance in the mirror. Shula had been right, she looked good. Her self confidence rose.

'Enjoy yourself!' Mary called after her as she left the apartment.

She luxuriated in the rare pleasure of walking through the town by herself just for the fun of it. Even if Harry Lyne did not appear, she would enjoy mixing with the crowds. When she reached the wide promenade she found that there were indeed many people strolling along by the sea, chatting idly to each other and greeting friends before going for a drink in one of the bars and cafés they passed.

Helen wandered slowly along, admiring the animated spectacle, pleasantly aware of approving looks from some of the promenaders. One or two young men smiled at her and she wondered what would happen if she smiled back.

It could be the start of a new adventure. She must be getting over the past!

Gradually she made her way towards the floodlit church which dominated the scene, pausing to admire the impressive sand sculptures of Neptune and a dragon which some unknown artist had painstakingly constructed in the hope that people would repay his work with coins tossed into the cardboard box which stood nearby.

'They're good, aren't they?' a voice said behind her, making her jump. It was Harry Lyne, fiery head crowning a broad smile.

'They are very good indeed,' Helen said appreciatively, fumbling in the pocket of her dress for a euro coin which she tossed into the box.

Harry fell into step beside her as she continued towards the church.

'This is my favourite bit of the town,' she confided. 'I love the church and the artists' houses near it — the ones which have been turned into museums. I wish

I could have a house with a balcony hanging over the sea.'

'Imagine it in winter with a gale blowing and the spray dashing against the windows,' he teased her.

When the promenade ended they wandered through the narrow streets, with Harry pointing things out and telling her stories about the artists who had lived there. He was obviously very proud of his adopted town. Gradually they came full circle and found themselves back by the sea.

When they both agreed it was time for a rest from walking, he steered her into a café, greeted the waiter in Spanish, and found them a table from which they could watch the passers-by.

'How long are you here for?' Harry asked casually, and Helen explained that she was half on holiday and half helping out Mary with the apartment. She explained Mary's situation.

'I'll have to be back in England for mid-September, but I'm not sure exactly when I'll go. It depends on when she begins to run out of clients.'

'She sounds a brave woman,' Harry said admiringly. 'I can understand her moving here, though. I came for a holiday and decided that this was where I wanted to live. It's not just the sun and the beaches — I like the people and the countryside, the history and the traditions.'

'What do you do here?'

'I write.'

She looked at him with renewed interest.

'Write what?'

'Well, when I first came about two years ago I intended to write a great novel. After a few months I realised I wasn't actually a great writer, however, so now I write short stories for various magazines and travel articles for others. I act as the local Spanish reporter for a couple of newspapers. I even translate instruction booklets from Spanish to English. When all else fails, I'm a pretty good handyman, and a lot of British residents like to have someone from home working for them.'

'It sounds as if you keep busy!'

He shrugged. 'Fairly busy. I earn enough to live on and I can take the occasional break when I want to and go walking in the mountains.'

They chatted idly for a bit longer, till Helen saw Harry watching her as she smothered a yawn.

'I'm sorry!' she apologised. 'The twins get us up very early, I'm afraid.'

'I know what it is like. When I visit my sister in England her three-year-old usually lands on my stomach about six o'clock in the morning. Definitely a rude awakening! Come on, I'll walk you back.'

When they reached the apartments Helen thanked him sincerely.

'I have enjoyed this evening. I've learned a lot about Sitges. Now I must try to creep in without waking Peter and Shula.'

'Good luck, and I look forward to seeing you again.'

She waved goodbye as he walked

away and turned towards the building, fumbling for her key. He hadn't suggested a specific time when they might meet again, which was a pity. Perhaps he didn't really want to meet her again? She shook her head angrily. Just because one man had rejected her didn't mean that every man would.

Once again there was a light in the living area downstairs. John Bridges was still up. She wondered what he was doing, and whether he felt lonely all by himself.

At breakfast the next morning Mary wanted to hear all about Harry Lyne, and was most impressed by the fact that he was a writer as well as a handyman.

'He's the kind of man who would make a success wherever he decided to move. He's sensible — he found out what was wanted.'

'You are doing the same thing,' Helen pointed out. 'You chose a place where tourists would want to rent an apartment, and you are making a success of it as well.'

'I'm surviving,' Mary said wryly. 'Now, what did you think of him as a possible boyfriend?'

Helen thought for a while, frowning slightly.

'I like him,' she admitted, 'but I like him in the way I like some of my brother's friends. I wouldn't mind seeing him again, but I won't be disappointed if I don't. He probably feels the same way, because he didn't make a definite date to meet again.'

'So there was no magic spark?'

Helen laughed. 'I'm sorry. No spark, no magic, just a pleasant evening.'

'Well, that's better than nothing.'

Once again Helen found herself reflecting that Mary was possibly growing bored with her limited horizons.

'John Bridges' lights were still on when I got back. I'll go down this morning and see if he will let me in to do the cleaning, or whether he's too busy with his criminal master plans.'

Later she clattered down the stairs armed with a bucketful of cleaning materials and knocked firmly on the door. There was a delay before John Bridges opened it and she braced herself for more acerbic comments, but instead he looked at her vaguely as if he had never seen her before.

'Yes?'

'I've come to clean the apartment,' she said crisply. 'You said I could only come in when you were here. Remember?'

He blinked uncertainly and then shuffled backwards so that she had room to enter. His trousers and shirt were rumpled and his hair stood up in random spikes as though he had been running his hands through it. Instead of resenting her intrusion, he seemed scarcely aware she was there.

'Er, there's not much to do,' he murmured as she strode into the kitchen and started filling the bucket.

'I'll do whatever is required. You can get on with whatever you are doing.'

He stood watching her for a minute as she wiped the table, and then wandered off towards the living area.

She worked her way briskly through the rooms, consciously making a little more noise than she would normally have done as if to impress on him that she was working at necessary tasks. She left the living area till last, and then marched in with her mop at the ready, but John Bridges remained unaware of her entrance. He was sitting in front of the computer, scowling blackly, and was actually tugging at locks of his hair as if he were trying to pull them out. He jumped visibly and spun round when she spoke.

'It is all right if I mop and dust in here?'

'You can leave this room,' he said abstractedly, turning back to the computer. Its screen was full of long lists of figures. She came closer, full of curiosity.

'Is everything all right?'

He was glaring at the computer again and she thought he was not going to reply. Then he sighed deeply.

'Would it break the contract if I

asked you to make me a cup of coffee instead of cleaning this room?'

An excuse to look inside the kitchen cupboards!

'Certainly not.'

Back in the kitchen she put on the kettle and found the cafetiere which Mary had supplied. It was easy to find the coffee. There was virtually nothing else in the cupboards except some biscuits and a packet of cereal. The refrigerator held an opened carton of milk, a packet of butter and a few eggs. The half-loaf in the breadbin was going stale. Thoughtfully she made the coffee and put the cafetiere on a tray with a mug. She poured some of the milk into a jug, hesitated, sniffed it, and then poured the milk down the sink. Then she carried the tray through to John Bridges.

'I couldn't find any sugar so I assume you don't take it. And you'll have to have it black because the milk has gone off.'

'It doesn't matter,' he said.

Coffee spilled on the tray as he tried to pour it into the mug without looking away from the computer. He seemed unaware that Helen continued to stand there until she coughed loudly, when he reacted by slamming down the lid of the computer.

'What do you want now?' he said irritably. The coffee seemed to have restored him to his normal bad-tempered state.

'When I made the coffee I couldn't help noticing that you have very little food. Would you like me to do some shopping for you? I could get fresh bread and milk, for example.'

He considered this offer and finally decided it was acceptable.

'I should be grateful if you would get me a few things. I did buy some oddments the other day, but I seem to have used them up. I don't want anything that needs cooking,' he added hastily, and his hand moved awkwardly towards his pocket. 'How much do you want?'

'I'll give you the bill when I come back.'

He nodded, but she could see his

thoughts were already turning else-where and he didn't seem to notice when she left.

Back upstairs, she explained to Mary that they would be shopping for one more person.

'That was a kind idea,' her friend said approvingly, 'especially when he's been so horrible to you.'

'Well, I couldn't let him starve. He must be one of those men who let their mothers or their girlfriends do all the shopping, so he hasn't a clue what to get.'

Mary fidgeted. 'You said he tried to hide the computer screen when you got close. What could you see?'

'Nothing but figures, as I said. There was nothing to indicate what they were about.'

'I still think it's very suspicious.'

'Mary, if he was doing something illegal he wouldn't be on his own. He'd have bodyguards with lots of muscle to look after him. At least, they do in the thrillers I read.'

'Perhaps he is a computer hacker

breaking into bank accounts! He could do that by himself.'

'You have an over-active imagination, Mary! Now let's get the twins ready and go shopping!'

An expedition to the local shops with the twins was always a time-consuming effort. The shopkeepers patted them, exclaimed at their good looks, and gave Mary suggestions on how children should be brought up in Spain. Peter and Shula revelled in all the attention and always came home with several small items which had not been on the shopping list. Helen accumulated a bagful of necessities for John Bridges and included several tins, deciding that heating soup or beans did not count as cooking.

Back at the apartment, she took the shopping down to him, and when he opened the door she carried the bag into the kitchen, set it down on the table so that she could give him the receipts she had been careful to collect, and started putting everything away while he went to find the money. He returned just as she was putting the tins in the cupboard.

'The tin opener is in that drawer,' she indicated.

'Thank you very much. You've obviously been to a lot of trouble.' He handed the money over, his eyes on the food. 'I suppose I am hungry. I've just been so preoccupied with other things that I didn't realise it.'

'Oh?' Helen said interrogatively, but he did not say any more and she left with her curiosity still unsatisfied.

3

The following morning Helen took herself off for a walk through the town, as she did occasionally when she had some free time. Mary encouraged this, saying it made her feel better about the enormous amount of work Helen did for her. This time she turned away from the sea and wandered through the narrow streets of the old town till she found the little museum which was housed in the nineteenth century mansion of a prosperous former citizen.

She had visited it before with the twins and had enjoyed the collection of dolls exhibited on one floor so much that she had resolved to come back and inspect them at her leisure. They were as beautiful and elaborate as she remembered, and afterwards she went on to inspect the rest of the house, and recognised a familiar red head peering into an impressive carriage. She hesitated, wondering whether to move away before Harry Lyne saw her, but it was too late. He straightened his back and greeted her with apparent pleasure and pointed to the vehicle.

'Which would you prefer? A modern car or this?'

She looked cautiously inside the carriage.

'I can imagine myself leaning back against the cushions in an elaborate dress while the coachman drove me through the town, but I don't think it would be as comfortable as a modern car for a long journey.'

He shrugged. 'I suspect you are right. The suspension doesn't look too good. Have you been looking round the museum?'

'Yes. I've been before but I came to see the dolls again.'

'That's a great collection,' he said enthusiastically. 'In fact I like all this museum.' He looked at her enquiringly. 'If you have seen it all, can I buy you a coffee now?'

She accepted the offer, which showed that at least he wasn't trying to avoid her, and as they left Harry waved goodbye to the ticket seller and said something in Spanish, which made the woman laugh.

'You sound like old friends,' Helen commented as they stepped out into the sunlight.

'Old acquaintances, at least. I give them publicity when I can in English tourist material, and in return they let me know when anything interesting is coming up in the cultural affairs of Sitges.'

'I wish I could speak Spanish as fluently as you do. I can understand what is said to me, but my accent is bad.'

He guided her to a pavement café and ordered coffee.

'I have enjoyed Sitges,' Helen said a little wistfully, looking around, 'but I would like the opportunity to have a good look around Barcelona. So far I have only seen it from the train when I passed through it on my way here.'

'You must go, and more than once,' he said firmly. 'Barcelona is beautiful and exciting, and it can take months to explore properly.'

'So I've been told. It is just that I feel I must help Mary all I can because she's had a very bad time and now she is trying very hard to make the apartment a success.'

'Suppose it doesn't work, what then?'

Helen bit her lip.

'Then she'd probably have to go to live with her parents, and I don't think that would work out very well. Her mother tends to tell other people what to do, and Mary is past the age of being ordered about.'

'She must be grateful for the help you have given her.'

Helen wrinkled her nose. 'She has helped me when I needed it.'

He waited for her to go on, but instead she looked at her watch and hurriedly pushed back her chair.

'I hadn't realised it was so late!

43

Thank you for the coffee, but I'd better get back now to help with lunch.'

'I'm going that way. Let me walk you back.'

It was a short five-minute stroll through streets already starting to empty for the long lunchtime which made the summer heat bearable.

'That's the house,' Helen pointed out, and then stopped and looked sharply at the building. 'Did you see that man standing by the house? He's gone round the corner now. I wonder if he's the repairman Mary has been expecting. The washing machine outlet has been flooding.'

But when they reached the house there was no-one in sight. Harry stood with his hands in his pockets, appraising the building.

'It's a well-built house in a good situation. With reasonable luck, your friend should do well.'

At that moment the door of the downstairs apartment opened and John Bridges came out. He hesitated at the sight of the two of them but then came towards them and greeted Helen politely, if without warmth.

'I decided to treat myself to lunch out,' he told her. 'In spite of your help, I am getting a little tired of soup.'

'There's a good restaurant in the first side street off the promenade,' Harry said. 'It doesn't look very impressive but the food is good.'

'Thank you, I might try it. My name's John Bridges, by the way, and you are . . . ?'

He raised his eyebrows interrogatively. It might have been an attempt at friendliness but it succeeded in sounding patronising.

'My name is Harry Lyne. I'm a journalist.'

John Bridge's face seemed momentarily to freeze, and then became expressionless.

'I see,' he said coldly. 'Well, goodbye.' Without another word he strode off rapidly. Helen stared after him.

'That was rude, even for him. What's

45

the matter with him?'

Harry was looking thoughtful. 'Either he doesn't like my name or my profession upset him. He didn't even wait for the details about the restaurant.'

'Helen!'

Mary was waving from the balcony.

'Lunch is ready!' She smiled down at Helen's companion. 'Would you like to join us, Mr Lyne?'

'Thank you, but I've got an appointment this afternoon. I'd better go home and spruce myself up.' He grinned up at Mary and his hand went up to stroke his fiery hair. 'I suppose I can guess how you recognised me.'

Mary was still giggling when Helen went up the stairs.

'I like your Harry,' she informed her friend. 'Why didn't you say you were going to meet him?'

'He's not my Harry, and I met him by accident,' Helen retorted. 'Incidentally, did the repairman call about the washing machine?'

46

Mary shook her head despondently. 'No, and the kitchen floor flooded again this morning.'

The rest of the day followed the usual routine. From time to time Helen wondered who the man standing by the gates had been. And why had Mr Bridges been so disturbed when he found that Harry Lyne was a journalist? She knew that to many people a journalist was a man who spent his time hunting out scandals. What did John Bridges want to keep secret? Had Mary been right when she said there might be something shady about his activities?

In the evening Mary checked her emails under Helen's supervision and discovered that her parents had altered their plans. They would now be coming to stay that weekend instead of the next because they had decided to bring forward one of their regular visits to England to see to business affairs and visit old friends.

'It will be nice to see them,' Mary said a little uncertainly.

'Of course it will!' Helen said warmly. 'You always worry about what they will think and then afterwards you say how much you enjoyed their company.'

'And I always say, 'Except for when Mother said . . . ' ' Mary reminded her.

'Well, this time she will have to be impressed by the way you are running the apartments.'

'So long as the washing machine doesn't flood the floor,' Mary said dolefully.

But this problem was to be solved. Soon after breakfast Helen took the twins to the beach while Mary got on with some cleaning. As she told Helen afterwards, some time later a little white van drew up outside the building and seconds later there was a knock on the door. Mary opened it to find Harry Lyne standing there smiling broadly and holding a large tool-bag.

'Good morning,' he said.

Mary smiled back uncertainly. 'Hello. I'm afraid Helen isn't here. She's gone to the beach with the children.'

'Actually I came to see you. Helen told me you were having trouble with your washing machine outlet. Did she tell you that I am an old-fashioned odd job man? I may be able to help.'

She threw the door wide. 'Welcome! If you can fix the machine before my parents arrive this weekend I shall be forever grateful.'

'Show it to me.'

When Helen brought the twins back she found Mary and Harry having coffee and obviously getting on very well. Mary rose to greet her.

'Harry's mended the washing machine outlet!'

Helen clapped her hands. 'No more flooded floors!'

'I'll get you some coffee, and then I'll give the twins a shower. I suppose they are covered with sand as usual.'

'I'll get myself some coffee if you will deal with the twins. They have brought half the beach back with them, as usual.'

'I'll do that. Harry's fixed that

49

annoying drip in the shower as well.'

Mary bustled the twins into the bathroom and Helen carried her cup of coffee into the lounge only to find Harry standing up and ready to leave.

'No time for a chat?' she commented, surprised.

'I'm afraid not. Somebody on the other side of town has phoned. They need my help with their wiring.'

'You mean I gave him a chance to talk to you and he just left?' Mary said after the twins had been showered and dried.

'He had to go somewhere,' Helen told her, aware of being slightly hurt. If Harry had had time for a cosy chat with Mary, surely he could have spared ten minutes for her? Oh well, she had already told Mary she wasn't interested in him romantically. Still, it was a nice change to have another adult to talk to occasionally.

She became aware that Mary was saying exactly the same thing.

'And he wouldn't let me pay him

anything. He said we small business people had to stick together and help each other.' She gave a surprisingly girlish giggle. 'I definitely like him.'

Helen was silent. She wondered if she would ever be able to enjoy flirting light-heartedly again, or whether the memory of George would always spoil everything. George had been in her group at university, and four months ago she had been convinced that they loved each other so deeply that she was going to spend the rest of her life with him. She had even jokingly arranged with her girlfriends who would be bridesmaids.

That was before George had sat her down one evening and said ruthlessly that he had met someone else and now realised that he had never really loved Helen. She had wept bitterly for her lost love, but facing her embarrassed and pitying friends had been even worse. She had been very grateful when Mary's invitation had given her a chance to get away from people who knew the sad little story.

Helen rose abruptly, deciding the subject should be changed.

'I'll go downstairs and see if Mr Bridges will let me clean the apartment again,' she announced.

Mr Bridges was in and told her she could do what she liked so long as she stayed out of the living room, to which he rapidly retreated, shutting the door firmly behind him. When she had cleaned the rest of the apartment and knocked to enquire whether he wanted any more shopping, he thanked her politely but said he did not need anything yet. She carried her bucket and mop up the stairs, brooding on the fact that no male under sixty seemed to want to talk to her.

The next day, Friday, was fully occupied with preparations for the visit by Mary's parents. At least they would not be staying at the apartment. They had done that once, but had found twenty-four hours in the company of Peter and Shula extremely exhausting.

Now they slept and had a leisurely breakfast in one of Sitges' many hotels before they arrived at Mary's after the twins had been fed, washed and dressed, and at the end of the day they retreated to their hotel when they had seen the twins bathed and put to bed.

'I do love my parents,' Mary assured Helen, 'and I know that if there was an emergency they would do everything in their power to help me. It's just that every time they come to visit I feel as if I were taking an exam in house craft and parenthood.'

'Well, I think you will pass with flying colours,' Helen said firmly as she ironed yet another pair of little shorts.

At the end of the afternoon Helen and Mary decided it was time to rest from their labours and sank down into comfortable chairs in the living room with a bottle of wine and two glasses on the coffee table between them. The flat was tidy, the twins were quietly building a tower with all their toys, roaring with laughter at its inevitable collapse before happily starting again, and the grandparents would be arriving the next day.

'Here's to us!' Mary said, lifting her glass in a toast. 'I think everything is ready.' Then she sat upright suddenly, spilling half her wine. 'No, it isn't! I haven't got any gin! They both like a gin and tonic before a meal! I'll have to go and buy a bottle!'

She put down her glass and began to stand up, but Helen was quicker.

'You stay here with the twins,' she ordered Mary. 'It won't take me five minutes to go to the shop.'

It did indeed take less than five minutes to reach the small local supermarket and pick up a bottle of gin and some tonics, but then it took another ten at the till while Senora Marquez asked how the twins were, and whether the apartment was let to the end of the summer, and how long Helen would be staying. It was more than twenty minutes therefore before Helen, hot and sweaty in the summer sun, returned to the apartment.

As she approached it she saw that once again there was a man by the gates, but this time she realised that he was in fact sheltering behind the hedge so that he could not be seen from the house. He was lurking, not waiting, and his attention was fixed on the house, so she was able to approach him before he realised it.

'Buenos dias,' she said sharply, and was gratified to see how he jumped and turned towards her in alarm.

'Do you want to speak to someone here?' she asked coldly, reverting to English. The man, tall and thin and about thirty-five, shook his head rapidly.

'I do not know this area. I am looking for a street,' he said in careful English.

'What street?'

He fumbled in his pocket as if looking for an envelope or map, then shrugged his shoulders.

'It does not matter. I will look another time,' he said, and walked rapidly away before she could interrogate him further.

She hoped she had scared him off but resolved to keep a look out for him. On reflection she decided not to tell Mary. There was no point in upsetting her unnecessarily when she was already worrying about her parents' visit.

4

The next morning she went to clean the downstairs apartment earlier than usual and found it empty but she decided that she would start anyway. If John Bridges raised a fuss when he came back and found her there, she would simply explain that she had started cleaning in his absence because she had to finish before Mary's visitors arrived, so when she heard the front door open she straightened up from cleaning the shower, took a deep breath, and went into the hall, wet cloth in hand.

'Mr Bridges . . . ' she began, and then stopped. The man with his hand on the door was not John Bridges but the man she had challenged outside the house the previous day! They stared at each other for a moment, and then he moved purposefully towards her. He looked menacing.

Thinking quickly, she threw the wet cloth at his face with all her force. It had the same effect as if she had slapped him hard across the face and temporarily blinded him and he was halted in his tracks. He tore the cloth away, but instead of advancing any further he turned and ran out of the front door into the street.

She ran after him, only to see him collide with John Bridges, who was walking towards the house carrying a plastic bag in each hand. Groceries were scattered over the pavement and as John Bridges hesitated over his shopping, staring after the man, the fugitive plunged down a side street into a maze of small streets where Helen knew it would be useless to try and follow him. John Bridges hastily stuffed his shopping back into the bags and then hurried to where Helen stood fuming outside the apartment.

'Who was that? What's happened?' he demanded.

'I think it was someone trying to

burgle you,' she told him, and quickly explained what had happened. John Bridges went straight into the living room but came out looking relieved.

'He didn't have the chance to take anything,' she told him crossly as he went to examine the lock on the front door.

'I know I locked it,' he said thoughtfully, 'and there's no sign of it being forced. He must have picked the lock. It is fairly basic.'

Reaction was making Helen feel shaky.

'We'd better call the police,' she said.

John Bridges looked at her sharply. 'No! Wait.'

'But it was a burglar!'

He took a deep breath, seemed to make a deliberate attempt to relax, and smiled at her.

'There's no point. Nothing is damaged and nothing has been taken, and the police will never catch the man.'

'But we ought to report it,' she said in amazement.

He looked at her steadily. 'Do you really want to get involved with the police when it won't serve any purpose? I don't want to waste time dealing with them and your friend won't want word to get round that your clients run the risk of being burgled.'

She hesitated at the idea of having to deal with an unfamiliar law system, and then thought of how Mary's parents would react if they arrived and found the house full of police. John Bridges saw her waver and held out his hand.

'Come on. Sit down while I check that everything is all right, and if it is, we will forget the incident.'

It took only five minutes to make sure that nothing in the apartment had been disturbed or taken.

'You see? Everything is all right. I doubt if there will be another attempt.'

Helen sighed. 'I suppose you are right. It would mean a lot of fuss, and that is the last thing Mary needs.' She jumped up. 'Mary will wonder what on earth has happened to me and I haven't cleaned here yet!'

'I'll survive. Now go and help your friend, and forget what happened here,' he said, gently urging her towards the door. 'You're a brave girl. No hysterics when you walked in on a burglar, and you've made a sensible decision.'

Helen made her way upstairs, vaguely aware that she had perhaps let herself be persuaded a little too easily.

'Is everything all right with our Mr Bridges?' Mary greeted her. 'You were a long time.'

'We got talking,' Helen said, deciding that if she told Mary about the burglar her friend would be very upset and would want to know why she hadn't told her about the man loitering around the apartments the previous day. It was simpler to keep quiet.

Mary commented on how preoccupied Helen was as she helped her prepare the salad.

'Mr Bridges wasn't unpleasant again, was he?'

Helen shook her head, but went on

brooding on the mystery of John Bridges.

Mary's parents, Mr and Mrs Loughborough, arrived just after Mary and Helen had fed the children, hastily changed Shula's dress when she dropped a generous amount of tomato sauce down it, and washed up the dishes. In fact, when the bell rang Mary almost dropped the casserole dish she was drying.

'They're here!'

'Good!' Helen said calmly, pulling her apron over her head. 'Remember, you are going to enjoy this visit.'

She knew the Loughboroughs well and they greeted Helen with affection as she let them in, but Mrs Loughborough was already looking up for her beloved grandchildren and soon there were delighted squeals as the twins unwrapped the presents she had brought them.

Her husband settled into a chair with a cup of coffee and before long had started to interrogate Mary quietly about the success of the apartments. Her replies seemed to satisfy him, and he was obviously impressed when she produced spreadsheets and financial calculations on the computer.

'Well, you are obviously being very business-like, and it all seems to be going satisfactorily, but remember you can always come to us if you have any trouble,' he told her.

'I know I can, but I don't want to impose on you,' Mary said gratefully.

Mr Loughborough nodded, but his lips tightened, and after a minute he sat up and leant forward.

'Mary, you wouldn't be imposing on us. We want to help; we want to be involved. I know you want to be independent, and I know your mother can be a little too eager to help, but we don't want to sit by knowing you are sometimes struggling to manage when we could make life easier for you. Don't let pride get in the way. If you need help, come to us.'

Mary's cheeks were flushed and her

eyes bright. She sat on the arm of her father's chair and kissed the top of his head. 'Thank you. I will remember that.'

'How are you, Helen?' Mrs Loughborough lowered her voice sympathetically. 'Have you got over George?'

It might sound like sheer nosiness, but Helen knew that Mrs Loughborough was good-hearted and really wished her well, so she managed a wry smile.

'What with the twins and helping Mary with the two apartments, I don't have time to think about past mistakes.'

'Have you met anybody else?'

Helen burst out laughing. 'Give me time!'

Foiled in her attempts to learn any secrets of Helen's love life, Mrs Loughborough turned her attention elsewhere.

'Who is in the apartment at the moment? Is it a family or a group of friends?'

'Neither. For some reason a Mister

John Bridges has it all to himself. We don't know why. He seems to spend all his time on the computer, as far as we can make out.'

Mrs Loughborough found this fascinating, and gave Helen the impression that she would somehow have found out more about the mystery man.

Lunch went well. Peter dropped ice cream down his T-shirt, but Mary whipped it off quickly and replaced it with a clean one. Peter was also experimenting with a novel method of dribbling water through his nearly-closed lips back into his glass until he encountered Helen's steely glare and decided it would be wise to stop.

Afterwards it was coffee on the balcony for the adults and while Mrs Loughborough was instructing Mary how to wash the dirty T-shirt, Helen glanced idly over the balcony wall and saw John Bridges walking along towards the house. Mrs Loughborough saw her expression change and stopped her discourse.

'What is it, Helen?' she enquired.

'Our Mr Bridges,' Helen told her grimly, and a second later Mrs Loughborough was leaning over the wall and waving at the tenant.

'Mr Bridges!' she called sweetly. 'I'm Mrs Loughborough, Mary's mother. She was coming down to introduce me later, but why don't you come up here now instead and have coffee with us?'

John Bridges halted and managed to produce a polite smile.

'Thank you, but I won't trouble you. I'm very busy, in fact I'm going to be very busy for the rest of the day, so if you will excuse me . . . '

Mrs Loughborough was ruthless. 'You can spare five minutes, I'm sure. Now come up, or I shall be very disappointed.'

John Bridges hesitated, but as he could not now have refused the invitation without downright rudeness, he climbed the stairs with obvious reluctance and was ushered into a chair while Mary found another cup for his coffee.

Mrs Loughborough opened her attack with the usual enquiries as to how Mr Bridges liked Spain and Sitges. His answers were polite but very brief.

'Mary says you are rattling about in the apartment all by yourself. Don't you feel lonely?'

'No,' was the firm answer.

'It must be a change from your life in England.'

This got only a tight-lipped smile and a nod, but Mrs Loughborough tried again. 'Helen says you spend all your time on your computer.'

'I spent a lot of time on it.'

Before Mrs Loughborough began to ask even more pointed questions her husband intervened, anxious to spare the young man any further interrogation about his person affairs.

'I have a laptop computer. I use it a lot for keeping in touch with England and dealing with house affairs. I'm a late beginner, however, and I do have problems.' He went on to describe some of the problems and John Bridges suggested some possible solution. Soon the two men were deep in technical discussions and Mrs Loughborough, foiled, could only listen.

John Bridges finished his coffee and put his cup down, then turned to Mary.

'Thank you, I've enjoyed meeting your parents. I wanted a word with you, anyway. I'll be away for the next two days, maybe longer. I'm going to Barcelona in the morning.'

'Fancy that!' said Mrs Loughborough brightly. 'Helen wants to see Barcelona and she could go tomorrow because we will be here to help Mary for the next two days.'

Helen simultaneously wished to sink into the earth and kill Mrs Loughborough! Didn't she realise how humiliating her blatant attempt to foist Helen onto John Bridges was? She gave him an agonised glance, but he simply said 'Really?' Then he stood up, turned to Mary, told her that he had to get back to work, and turned purposefully towards the door.

'I'll see you out,' Helen said hurriedly,

and accompanied him to the apartment's front door.

'I'm sorry!' she hissed quietly. 'She means well, believe me!'

For the first time, John Bridges broke into a spontaneous smile.

'Don't worry. I've got an aunt just like her.'

She smiled at him gratefully. For a moment they looked at each other with new eyes, and then he turned away and went down the stairs.

Later, Mary found an opportunity to draw Helen aside for a quiet word.

'You know, it's true what she said. This is your chance to go to Barcelona, without that horrible man, of course.'

'Let me think about it.'

It didn't take much thought. She wasn't needed in Sitges during the family reunion. Mrs Loughborough would love the chance to help look after the children and the apartment, and it might be Helen's only opportunity to get away for two days in Barcelona. She told Mary she would like to go, so they telephoned and booked a night at a quiet hotel which had been recommended to them, and all Helen had to do was pack an overnight bag.

It was nearly lunchtime before she arrived in Barcelona and found her hotel near the great Plaza de Espana, the square which separated the old and new towns.

With her guide book gripped firmly in her hand, she returned to the square and spent the afternoon sitting on one of the tourist buses, gazing with interest at the various sights as the bus drove round the city and deciding which ones she would visit the next day. Her hotel provided breakfast but no evening meal, so after a quick trip back there to freshen up and change, Helen stepped out to find some food.

Now she began to miss having a companion. Barcelona was big, noisy and bustling with thousand of people, all of whom seemed to be happily chatting to someone else. Helen felt intimidated, but she drew a deep breath, squared her shoulders, and set out into the crowds.

She decided to walk down the famous Las Ramblas, the wide street that linked the Plaza d'Espana to the sea front, knowing there had to be plenty of restaurants and snack bars in an area crammed with tourists. Soon she had forgotten her solitary state and was gazing open-mouthed at flower-stalls filled with exotic blooms and living statues that moved abruptly just when you least expected it.

'Vaya!' a voice said angrily behind her, and she spun round to see John Bridges confronting a teenager who backed away from him before turning and vanishing into the crowd, leaving Helen wondering what on earth was happening.

'What's the matter? Why did you shout at that boy?' she demanded, and John Bridges pointed at her handbag, hanging from her shoulder by a slender strap.

'If you check, you'll see that he had

managed to slide the zip of your bag open. If I hadn't seen him and shouted at him he would have had your purse out within seconds.'

Helen's hand flew to her bag and she found that was indeed half-open.

'Don't you realise that where there are tourists there are always pickpockets?' John Bridges continued. She felt like a schoolchild being lectured.

'I'm sorry! I didn't realise . . . Thank you,' she said in confusion.

'Well, take more care from now on,' he admonished her. 'Now, do you want any help? Do you know where you are going?'

'I will take care and I don't need help. Thank you again,' Helen said with dignity. Eager to get away from him, she stepped off the pavement, and would have been mown down by a car which sounded its horn angrily if John Bridges had not seized her by the arm and pulled her back just in time.

'Cars drive on the right in Spain,' he

said grimly. 'Haven't you learned that in Sitges?'

A narrow escape from a pickpocket and from being run over by a car had left Helen speechless. Her saviour's expression softened a little.

'Barcelona takes some adjusting. What are you doing actually?'

'I am trying to find somewhere to eat,' she managed. 'I missed lunch, so I'm hungry.'

He sighed resignedly 'Come on. I know somewhere where we can eat.'

'I am capable of finding somewhere by myself, thank you,' she said defiantly, indicating the chairs and tables set out on the pavements.

'Tourist traps,' said John Bridges dismissively. 'They serve cheap food at high prices, just because they are on Las Ramblas. Come with me.' She looked at him uncertainly, and suddenly he smiled. 'Look, if you end up penniless and suffering from food poisoning, the formidable Mrs Loughborough will hold me responsible.'

She returned his smile uncertainly. 'In that case, provided we both understand that if we hadn't met I would have been able to cope perfectly well, I accept your invitation.'

'With that understood, and your pride saved, let us cross the road — carefully,' he replied.

He conducted her to a pleasant square off Las Ramblas and they were soon seated at a table which gave them a good view of the passers by. John Bridges addressed the waiter in fluent Spanish, and soon coffee and long rolls filled with ham and cheese appeared.

'You must know that self-respecting restaurants in Barcelona don't serve proper meals till the late evening,' he pointed out as she looked at them with a trace of disappointment. The coffee and food did take the edge off her hunger, however, and she began to relax.

'Now, tell me what you have done today and what your plans are,' he instructed her, and she told him about the tourist bus ride. He nodded approvingly.

'That was a good start. The tourist buses are a very good way of getting a general view of Barcelona.'

'Tomorrow I want to go back and see a couple of houses and that fantastic church, La Sagrad Familia, in the morning, and in the afternoon I can see some of the museums in the old city.'

He held up a warning hand. 'Stop! Don't try and see all Barcelona in a day. It's impossible. I've been here plenty of times and I'm still discovering new things. Choose one or two sights and see them properly. What were you planning for this evening?'

'After I'd eaten? I was going to walk down to the port and then go back to my hotel.'

He gazed at her incredulously. 'Go back to your hotel? Do you realise that there are places in Barcelona which don't open till the early hours of the morning?' He shook his head in disbelief and sighed deeply. 'I can't let you do it. This evening I shall personally escort you round the old city.'

Helen remembered for an instant how much she had wanted a companion, and then remembered who she was with. She might be grateful to him for saving her money and her life, but she still didn't like him.

'Mr Bridges . . . '

'As we were going to spend the evening together, please call me John.'

Short of getting up and running away, there seemed no way of escape and she resigned herself to the inevitable.

'My name is Helen.'

'I know. I have heard those awful twins calling you — usually very early in the morning.'

She decided to defend Peter and Shula another time.

'So what do we do next?' she asked instead.

'We wander.' He rose and held out his hand. 'Come on.'

5

They wandered. They drifted with the crowd along Las Ramblas and saw the sea. They wandered into a museum where holograms recreated the ghosts of sailors fighting an ancient sea battle. Then they found a café flaunting its Art Deco glass and had wine and tapas, the little savouries that Spaniards consume so readily.

When they emerged night had fallen and floodlit buildings loomed over the crowds like dramatic backdrops in some enormous theatre. Once the great cathedral stood over them, then they found themselves in the Plaza España with the fountains dancing like white flames. At one point they stared up at a building where dramatic lighting had transformed the balconies into skulls below a roofscape shaped like a crouching dragon.

Helen was entranced, and was almost reluctant to leave the streets when John told her firmly that it was now time for dinner. Back in the old town, however, she realised how hungry she was and relished the tiny grilled squids in garlic butter and then the tender lamb which was ordered for her.

John poured her another glass of wine.

'Tell me, why are you in Spain acting as maid-cum-mother's help?' he asked curiously.

She explained Mary's situation.

'I was at school with her and we've been friends ever since, so when I needed to escape she offered me the chance to come here.'

'To escape from what?' he pounced.

It must have been the extra glass of wine, but she found herself confiding in him.

'I fell in love, but the man decided he didn't love me.'

'More fool him,' John commented, and she felt strangely comforted. 'What about your journalist friend?'

'Harry? Oh, he is just a friend. We met on the beach and we've only met a couple of times. Anyway, he's not really a journalist. He does some writing about tourism, but he's also a plumber and general handyman.'

He seemed pleased. 'So, he's not important to you?'

She shook her head.

For a moment he seemed to forget her as he frowned down at his wine glass. Then he looked up and gave a bleak smile.

'You know, you probably had a lucky escape when that man told you he didn't love you, no matter how much it hurt at the time. I fell in love once, and I didn't find out she didn't love me until it was too late.' He shook his head as if to dispel bad memories. 'Let's forget the past and enjoy ourselves.'

It was a magical evening, but as coffee was served she found her eyelids drooping. She saw John Bridges watching her, smiling and she shrugged.

'I'm sorry. It has been a very full day.'

'I understand. Come on, which hotel did you say you were staying at?'

Back at her hotel, he waited while the receptionist gave her the room key.

'Good night, Helen. Sweet dreams.'

'Good night, and thank you. It was a marvellous evening.' She looked at him a little wistfully. 'Shall I see you tomorrow?'

He shook his head. 'I'm afraid I shall be busy all day. I'll see you back in Sitges.'

She smiled a little sadly.

'Then thank you once again for showing me something of Barcelona as it should be seen.'

'It was a pleasure, and I hope you enjoy tomorrow.'

Then he was gone, walking briskly out of the door, and she went up to her room almost reluctantly. It seemed a tame, downbeat ending to such a wonderful evening, but how else could it have ended? She would see him again in Sitges, but it would not be the same.

She would be the maid, the cleaner, and he would be the impatient tenant.

Helen spent the following morning dutifully viewing some of the remaining sights of Barcelona while looking both ways when crossing the roads and keeping a tight hold on her handbag. The city was thrilling and beautiful, but she missed having someone to share her wonder at the architecture and eccentricities, and it was probably for this reason, as well as her tired feet, that she collected her bag from her hotel earlier than she had intended and caught a train that got her back to Sitges in the late afternoon.

The family welcomed her warmly, but she was a little surprised to see Harry Lyne sitting on the roof terrace with the Loughboroughs like an old friend of the family.

'I was passing, so I thought I'd check whether the washing machine was still all right,' he explained. 'Then Mr Loughborough and I got talking.'

'Well, I told him how Mary wanted

a swimming-pool for the downstairs apartment but couldn't afford to have one put in.'

'It can be very expensive if you go to one of the contractors who specialise in putting them into holiday homes, but it can be a lot cheaper if you buy the materials and find the workmen yourself, and I could do that for her,' Harry informed her.

Mr Loughborough nodded approvingly.

'We've already sketched out some plans. Now, how did you enjoy your trip to the big city?'

It was pleasant to relax and tell her friends about Barcelona, though she found herself playing down her evening with John Bridges, somehow giving the impression that she had seen him only briefly and had just exchanged a few words with him.

Harry was frowning. 'I've got a feeling I've seen Mr Bridges somewhere before, or at least a photograph of him. It can't have been anything exciting or I would have remembered.'

When evening approached the group finally broke up and Helen saw Harry to the door. He hesitated as she opened it for him.

'Is there any chance of seeing you on the front this evening?'

She was flattered, but shook her head reluctantly. 'I'm sorry, but after two days of looking round Barcelona I'm too tired.'

'That's a pity. I thought that you could have brought Mary with you, as her parents are here to babysit. Apparently she's never seen the promenade at night.'

Helen stopped feeling so flattered. Harry definitely seemed more concerned with Mary than with her. This impression was reinforced by Mrs Loughborough when she took Helen aside for 'a little talk' while Mary was seeing to the children.

'We're so pleased to see Mary coping so well with the apartments,' she began. 'Of course, having you here has made things easier for her. I'm not sure how she will manage without you.'

This sounded like emotional blackmail. 'I'm afraid I will have to go back to England to start my teacher-training course in a few weeks,' Helen said firmly.

'Of course, my dear. You must think of yourself,' Mrs Loughborough said soothingly, and Helen immediately began to feel guilty. 'Fortunately it looks as if she will have someone to turn to,' the older woman continued. 'She and Mr Lyne seem to be getting on very well together.'

Helen became uncomfortably aware that Mrs Loughborough had her gimlet eyes fixed on her intently, as though waiting for some reaction.

'That's good,' she managed to say. 'He seems a very practical, useful man.'

'Exactly. And he is on his own, so he can come over at any time.'

Helen kept silent.

'Mary did say that you had met him once or twice and liked him, but that was all.' The implied question was very clear, and Mrs Loughborough waited for an answer.

'Mary was right,' Helen said. 'I would like to think we are friends, but that is all. After all, in a few weeks I'll be leaving Sitges.'

'Just what I said to Mary!' beamed her proud mother. She patted Helen's arm. 'I'm glad we've got that straight. After all, I'm sure you'll meet some nice young man eventually — though schools seem to be full of women teachers nowadays.'

Helen gritted her teeth and went to do the washing-up. At least everyone agreed that she was useful!

Halfway through the next day, Mary was chatting to Helen as they cleared up after lunch. The twins were napping, and the Loughboroughs were dozing on the terrace. Mary made some remark, waited for an answer, and saw that Helen was not paying attention.

'Helen! What's the matter? It's clear you're not listening to a word I'm saying,' she complained, obviously half-irritated and half-amused.

Her friend blinked and then apologised. 'I'm sorry. I was thinking of something.'

'That was obvious. What's the matter?' Mary's eyes widened. 'Mother hasn't said something tactless again, has she?'

Helen shook her head. 'No, nothing like that. I was just thinking how sorry I shall be to leave Spain when the time comes. I know that taking this teacher training course is the practical thing to do. It's just that I'm not sure I really want to be a teacher, but I can't think of anything else I do want to do.'

Mary put away some clean plates. 'I was wondering about that. Your decision did seem a bit sudden, and you've never talked about wanting to be a teacher before.'

'You mean before George dumped me?' Helen asked wryly. 'I suppose I was just drifting along with the vague dreams of marriage and children. I didn't really think I'd need a proper career. Well, I'll take the course and see how I get on. It might turn out that I'll be very happy teaching.' She decided to change the conversation. 'I haven't heard any noise from downstairs. Mr Bridges can't have got back from Barcelona yet. Next time I see him I'll thank him for his help in Barcelona.'

'You seem to like him more than you did.'

'I don't dislike him quite as much, anyway. I have a theory that he is one of those men who are so wrapped up in their work that they can't think of anything else till they have finished a task. Perhaps he was so unfriendly when he first arrived because all he wanted to do was work on his computer.'

Later that afternoon the quiet day erupted into high drama. Peter woke up full of energy and with only his grandparents for audience insisted on showing his grandfather how high he could jump on the couch. Unfortunately he slipped as he landed from one particularly high effort and fell off the couch, striking his head on the corner of the coffee table. He gave a piercing scream, and Mary and Helen rushed in to find Mr and Mrs Loughborough trying to comfort a child with blood steaming down his face while his sister was giving panic-stricken shrieks.

'There's a clinic five minutes' drive away,' said white-faced Mary. 'Dad, you drive us there.'

'I'm coming too,' insisted Mrs Loughborough.

Mary nodded. 'Of course you are. Helen, will you stay here and look after Shula?'

In an amazingly short space of time the car drew away with Mary holding her son in her arms and Helen was left to comfort Shula. An hour later the car returned. Peter had a plaster on his forehead and had obviously recovered from the shock and was beginning to enjoy the attention he was receiving.

'When all the blood was cleared away it was a surprisingly small cut,' Mary told Helen. 'He'll probably have a magnificent black eye tomorrow, but with a little luck he's going to be fine. My parents are feeling very guilty. They feel it was their fault.' She giggled. 'They certainly wouldn't have let me jump on their couch!'

There was still no light in the downstairs apartment when Helen went to bed that night. John Bridges must have found Barcelona more interesting.

Whether it was the accident or the call of their own home, the following morning Mr and Mrs Loughborough announced that they had decided to leave that day.

'Can't you stay another day?' Mary asked. 'The children love having you here.'

'Even after that?' said Mrs Loughborough, pointing at Peter's impressive black eye.

Mary hugged her mother. 'Don't be silly. All children take appalling risks. Anyway, Peter is very proud of that black eye. He thinks it makes him look like a pirate.'

Privately she told Helen that she thought her parents had been more shocked by the accident than Peter and needed to go home and recover. Mrs Loughborough particularly seemed very subdued, her faith in her own infallibility obviously shaken. Mary persuaded them to stay till late afternoon, anyway, so there was time for a last walk along the beach and lunch at a small restaurant which welcomed the children gladly.

The Loughboroughs were obviously somewhat reassured by their grandchildren's reluctance to part with them, and there were tears on both sides before they finally drove off, promising to come again soon. Helen and Mary retreated to the terrace for a cup of coffee, but the children were fretful and restless, inclined to quarrel with each other.

After breaking up one shrill-voiced disagreement, Mary decided to combine distracting them with a necessary errand and announced that she was going to take them to a hypermarket for a big shop and it was dark when a taxi finally deposited the group and their purchases back at the apartment.

'I shall be in bed early tonight,' sighed Mary, and turned to Helen, who was staring at the downstairs windows. 'What is the matter?'

'Look, there are lights on. Mr Bridges must be back.'

Mary yawned, completely uninterested. 'Well, he's allowed. He's rented the place.'

Helen followed her upstairs, frowning. She must have been mistaken, but there had been an instant when she had thought she had seen two silhouettes in the downstairs windows.

It was eleven o'clock the next morning when she collected her pail, mop and dusters and made her way down. To her own annoyance, she had found herself wondering what to wear and whether she should put some make-up on. After all, John Bridges had seen her dressed up for Barcelona, and jeans and a T-shirt were definitely not very attractive.

Then she wondered why on earth she wanted to wear attractive clothes for John Bridges. Resolutely she clattered down the steps, with her hair scraped back from a face innocent of as much as a touch of lipstick. She knocked, waited for a couple of seconds, opened the door and marched in.

'I'm here to do the cleaning,' she announced loudly, and then stopped dead as a bedroom door opened and a stranger appeared. It was a woman, dressed in silky robe draped casually over a brief, lacy nightdress which revealed a stunning figure. Dark hair tumbled round a face with big dark eyes and pouting lips.

Helen gulped. 'I'll come back some other time,' she managed to croak, but the woman raised a languid hand.

'Wait a second. I wanted to speak to someone about the shower. It takes ages to reach a tolerable temperature. Will you please tell whoever is responsible to have it fixed?'

Helen nodded automatically, then managed to say, 'Mr Bridges hasn't complained.'

The vision lifted a thin eyebrow. 'But I am Mrs Bridges, and I am complaining.'

As Helen was digesting this information the kitchen door opened and John Bridges appeared in dressing-gown and pyjamas, holding two cups of coffee. The woman laid a possessive hand on his arm.

'John, darling, I've asked the maid to get the shower mended. Do you agree?'

John Bridges, obviously embarrassed, managed a brief nod and rapidly vanished into the refuge of the kitchen. The woman smiled at Helen with acid sweetness.

'You can come back to clean about two o'clock. John will be taking me to lunch then.'

Helen was fuming when she returned to Mary. 'We were right in the first place. He's a horrible man! How dare he? He can't just import strange women when he feels like it! You'll have to speak to him!'

'Hold on!' Mary held up her hand. 'He rented the apartment and he can have whoever he wants to stay there, and this is his wife! I'm glad she has appeared. It looks like she was supposed to come with him all the time. Perhaps she had to stay behind for a reason, perhaps they had an argument. Anyway, I'm glad she is here. It shows I was worrying over nothing. He just wanted the apartment for a holiday with his wife.'

Just before two they heard a door open and shut and were in time to see John Bridges escorting the new arrival down the road towards the restaurant area of the town. Mrs Bridges was teetering along on high heels and wearing a very skimpy sundress. Helen, still seething, had to forego her quiet after-lunch rest and hurry downstairs so that the apartment would be clean and tidy when the Bridges returned.

It did not help her mood when she found dirty cups, toast crumbs and smears of melting butter on the work surfaces while the milk had been left out of the refrigerator. The bathroom was even worse. Cosmetics and toiletries covered all the flat surfaces, and a wet bath towel had been abandoned on the floor. Grimly Helen tidied and scrubbed, then made for the master bedroom, where two large open cases spilled clothes.

Well, Mrs Bridges could hang her own clothes up, Helen decided. Then she took another look at the room. The bedclothes had been flung carelessly aside on one of the twin beds, and the indented pillow showed where a head had rested. But the other bed was untouched. Thoughtfully Helen opened the door of the second bedroom, and saw that one of the beds there had been slept in, though the bedclothes had been straightened.

So the Bridges had not shared a

room — or had not stayed together for the whole night, Helen corrected herself. Maybe John Bridges had been banished to another room because he snored. There were several possible explanations. Still, it was interesting.

6

Mary was on the phone upstairs. 'Yes, I would be grateful. This afternoon? If it's convenient. I'll see you then.' She turned to Helen. 'Harry says he'll call and look at the shower today. It's very kind of him.'

She listened while Helen told her what she had found downstairs, but seemed a little abstracted.

'A mess? What a pity! Still, she can't be as bad as the last lot.' She looked in the mirror and bit her lip. 'Could you keep an eye on the twins for half-an-hour? I think I could do with a shower and changing this old dress.'

She reappeared in a fairly new dress and Helen could detect unfamiliar traces of make-up. Mary reaped her reward when Harry Lyne appeared and complimented her on her appearance.

'I've just freshened up for the

afternoon,' she protested, blushing like a schoolgirl. 'Anyway, I can't thank you enough for coming so soon. I'm not sure if the Bridges are back or not.'

'Yes, they are,' Helen informed her, pointing down at the lawn. Mrs Bridges, now dressed in a very skimpy bikini, was sunbathing on a blanket spread on the grass. 'She's taken that off one of the beds. It shouldn't be outside,' she commented sternly, but saw that Harry had not heard her. He was too busy gazing down at the sunbather. Mary noticed this as well, and her lips tightened.

'Perhaps you would like to go and ask if you can look at the shower now,' she said a little sharply. Harry, recalled to duty, did as she directed and reappeared about thirty minutes later.

'The thermostat needed a little attention, that was all,' he told them. 'I've fixed it.'

Mary sighed with relief. 'Thank you. How much do I owe you?'

'Nothing,' he said firmly.

'But I must pay you! You can't go on doing jobs for me for nothing.'

'I'll settle for a cup of tea and a biscuit,' he assured her. This, together with some pleasant chat, occupied the next hour, though Mary was still worried.

'I do a lot of my writing and research in the evening, so I like to relax in the afternoon, and I enjoy spending time with two pretty women,' he told her, and she accepted this reassurance.

Harry did make one comment, which Helen noted.

'When I went downstairs your Mr Bridges was reading in the lounge but he gave me one look and disappeared into the bedroom, leaving his wife to show me what needed doing. He seemed a bit gloomy. If I had a good-looking wife like that I'd be overjoyed when she reappeared after we'd been separated.'

He realised that both women were looking at him coldly, and fell tactfully silent. Later Helen decided to put a plan she had thought of into action.

'Harry, I was telling Mary how much you told me about Sitges the other night. If I baby-sit the children tonight, could you show her round the town?'

Harry's face lit up. 'I'd be delighted!'

'No, I couldn't,' protested Mary. 'You said you usually work in the evening.'

'But this evening I've got to report on a concert in one of the artists' houses. Come with me, and then we can have a walk round afterwards — if you would like to.'

Mary's cheeks were red. 'I'd like to very much,' she said shyly.

'Good!' Harry stood up. 'Then I'll pick you up about seven.'

When he had gone Mary turned to Helen.

'That was embarrassing! You practically forced the poor man to say he would take me out!'

'And aren't you glad I did?' Helen returned.

Mary fell silent, looked at the floor, then gave a little smile. 'Perhaps I am.'

A frown replaced the smile. 'Do you mind?'

Helen sighed impatiently. 'Mary, how many times do I have to tell you that I like Harry Lyne — but as a friend, that's all.'

'Good!' The frown returned. 'Helen, what shall I wear?'

Helen was fast asleep when Mary came back that night, so she interrogated her over breakfast.

Mary seemed to have acquired a permanent gentle smile. 'I don't know what the concert was like,' she confessed. 'I was too nervous. But afterwards we walked along by the sea for a bit and then we went for coffee. We just sat and talked and it was as if we had known each other for years. It was marvellous. I could be myself with him — Mary, a widow with two young children.'

'With a lot of life left to enjoy,' Helen said softly, and received a radiant smile.

'Do you know, for the first time since Dave died I began to feel that. Well, this may come to nothing and Harry and I may settle for just being friends, but at least I feel now that I do have a life to live and that I don't have to spend years just remembering the past. And I think that would please Dave.'

Mary insisted that Helen should have some free time to make up for her babysitting duties the previous evening, so mid-morning Helen wandered off towards the seafront. She had decided it would be pleasant exercise to walk the full length of the promenade. She was distracted, however, by the sand sculptor, who was busy adding a mermaid and a dolphin to his work.

'Did you enjoy Barcelona?' said a voice near her, and when she turned sharply she saw that the speaker was John Bridges, leaning against the seawall.

'I loved it!' she assured him. 'Thank you for your help and information. It helped me a lot.' She gave a carefully casual look around. 'Isn't Mrs Bridges with you?'

He took a deep breath and gritted his teeth. 'No. The former Mrs Bridges, the ex-Mrs Bridges, the woman who was once Mrs Bridges but is so no longer, has stayed in the apartment.'

She stared at him, taken aback by his outburst, and he gave a shamefaced laugh and stood upright.

'I apologise. I've had a rough couple of days and I'm in a thoroughly bad temper.'

'I'm sorry.'

'So am I.' He half-turned, as if to leave without any more conversation, but then turned back to her as if a thought had just occurred to him. 'If you are prepared to walk along the promenade with me for a while it will give me a chance to explain. I think I would feel better if I could talk to someone.'

There was an unexpected note of pleading in his voice. Helen decided it would be unkind to reject this call for help, and anyway she was full of curiosity. They fell into step together.

'Do you remember that I told you in Barcelona that I once fell in love and found out too late that she didn't love me? That was Michelle. It was my own fault. Other men my age had led a normal social life and learned something about women. I'd spent years doing nothing except concentrate on building up my career and at twenty-eight I was still naïve and inexperienced. Then I met Michelle, and I fell for her hard.'

'She is very attractive,' Helen ventured.

'Seven years ago she was the most beautiful woman I had ever met, and she was charming and flattering as well. I wouldn't listen to any warning from friends who told me to take things slowly. I asked her to marry me a couple of weeks after we met, she accepted, and we were married as soon as possible. I suppose I was happy for a week before Michelle began to realise that I might have a promising future, but I hadn't actually got a lot of money.

'She soon made it clear that she felt I

had deceived her and that she wouldn't have married me if she hadn't thought I was rich. After that, it was just a question of how quickly she could get a divorce.'

'But if you are no longer married,' Helen said, puzzled, 'what is she doing here?'

'We parted fairly amicably. I was just glad to see her go by the end. Now, if she's run out of money or is between boyfriends, she sometimes arrives on my doorstep and takes it for granted that I will help her or put her up till something better comes along.' He frowned. 'I'm still trying to work out how she knew I was in Barcelona. She just knocked on my hotel room and said she needed somewhere to stay for a few days. When I asked her how she knew I was there she just said someone had told her. I thought I'd managed to keep my stay here a deep secret.'

Helen was shaking her head. 'I don't understand why you didn't just tell her to go away.'

'If I'd met someone else or got married I suppose I would, but I did love her once for a short time, until I found what she was really like, and in a way I feel sorry for her. All her life she has used her looks and her charm to get her what she wants, but she is getting older now and the last few times we've met I have felt that she was getting worried and a little frightened about her future.' He managed a smile. 'Anyway, thank you for listening. It has made me feel a bit better. Now tell me what you did in Barcelona by yourself.'

Clearly he had decided they had spent enough time on Michelle Bridges. Helen gave him a brief account of her city exploration.

'Of course, I want to go back and see more,' she finished.

'Of course. There is always more to see in Barcelona. Won't the man who mended my shower and also claims to be a journalist take you?'

'Oh! You mean Harry Lyne. It looks as if he prefers Mary.'

'I'm surprised,' was all he said, which she decided could be interpreted as a compliment.

They had turned back some time ago and were now approaching the apartments.

'Michelle will be waiting to go out for lunch. She doesn't cook, of course. Can you give me the names of a few restaurants so that we can try different places? The information file lists restaurants suitable for families, and those aren't Michelle's style.'

'I'll think of a few and bring details down tomorrow when I come to clean.'

They had reached Mary's building.

'Thank you,' he said.

'It's no trouble. I'm sorry the list in the information pack is not adequate.'

'I'm not talking about the restaurants. Thank you for listening, for being patient with me when I haven't always behaved very pleasantly towards you.'

There was no more to say, and as he let himself in his door Helen hurried up the stairs to tell Mary what she had learned. Mary, of course, felt sympathy for both the Bridges.

'Do you think she will stay till John Bridges goes?'

'I've no idea. Anyway, you can forget your idea of him as a master criminal. Anyone who is so kind to an ex-wife is definitely not ruthless enough.'

'That doesn't necessarily follow. He may be ruthless with men but weak with women.'

'No, I've changed my mind about him. I quite like him now. Anyway, it will be interesting to see how they are behaving towards each other when I go down tomorrow with clean bedding and towels.'

Helen was disappointed, however. When there was no response to her knock she assumed the apartment was empty and she used her key to open the door, then, with her arms full of linen, kicked it shut with her foot. Immediately there was a clattering sound and Michelle Bridges backed out of the broom cupboard next door to the kitchen.

Helen explained her errand to the flustered Michelle and went to collect the dirty linen from the bedrooms. She was surprised when Michelle followed her.

'Can I help you?'

'I was looking for something — a book. My husband must have picked it up with his papers. Do you know where he keeps things like that?'

Helen found it difficult to imagine the glamorous Michelle absorbed in a book and couldn't understand why the woman had to ask her about John's habits. And why had she been looking for a book in the broom cupboard? Michelle obviously saw the bewilderment and shrugged.

'It doesn't matter. I'll ask him when he comes back.'

In the clear light of the morning sun it was possible to see that Michelle was older than she appeared at first sight. There were shadows under her eyes and fine lines at the corner of her eyes and mouth. Confident in her own youth and ability, Helen felt an irritating mixture of compassion and impatience towards her.

'Tell me the title, and I may find it when I am cleaning.'

'It's not that important,' Michelle said a little snappishly. 'I'm going to sunbathe.'

She flounced off to the sunlit lawn, leaving Helen free to get on with her work.

Back upstairs, Helen heard that Mary had just received a phone call from her mother in England.

'They had a smooth flight back,' she reported, 'but it is raining heavily and she says she is missing Spain already. However, she always goes back with a long shopping list and she'll forget the weather as soon as she hits the shops. Did you ask her to do you something for you? She said she was going to see your parents and hoped to do you a favour.'

Helen looked blank. 'No. I wonder what she meant. It's a bit worrying, though. I know she's your mother, Mary, but you do appreciate that her idea of a favour might not be mine.'

'I do understand. If she calls again I'll try to find out what she meant.'

'And tell her not to bother.'

The rest of the day was as tranquil as it could be with two young active children to keep them occupied, but evening brought Harry Lyne knocking at the door, his face shining with excitement and with a file of papers under one arm.

'I've been doing some research on the internet,' he announced, 'and I've found out who your tenant, John Bridges, really is.'

He scattered pages of computer printout over the table.

'First of all, he's really David Bridges — John is his second name. Look!'

He pointed at a photograph. John Bridges was recognisable; one of a small group of men formally dressed in suits and ties.

'This is at some business conference. He only seems to be photographed at similar events.'

'But what does he do?'

Harry scratched his head.

'I've been trying to sort things into date order. As far as I can make out, he started as a business consultant, advising people how to organise firms efficiently. Then he started investing in the firms, taking blocks of shares instead of a fee so he benefited when the firms became more profitable. He seems to have done well. Look what this one says.' He pointed at one photograph. 'David Bridges, millionaire businessman, discussing current affairs in the City.'

'Millionaire?' Mary's eyes were wide. 'Why did he come to my apartment then?'

Harry shrugged. 'That's the question. He doesn't seem to throw money about, but I would have expected him to rent a private villa at least.'

'It is interesting,' Helen said slowly, 'but I suppose the fact that he's rich doesn't mean anything to us. He's just another client who needs the bathroom cleaned and his sheets changed.'

'It might make a difference to me,' Harry said eagerly. 'If he's come here for some special reason there might be a story in it for me. I could sell news about Mr Bridges to the national papers. Has he had any visitors?'

'Only Michelle, and he told Helen about her.'

She gave him a quick account of the unexpected Mrs Bridges, and a slow grin appeared on his face.

'Even the fact that she's reappeared in his life would interest some papers.'

'Wait a minute!' Helen said urgently. 'You can't sell information about him. He's here as Mary's client, almost her guest. How many people do you think would rent the apartment if they heard that anything Mary learned about them might be splashed all over the papers?'

Mary looked taken aback but Harry shook his head.

'How many millionaires are likely to come here?' he demanded, then looked at Helen's thunderous face. 'All right, maybe I shouldn't sell gossip, but there may be an important story that should be made public.'

The discussion went on for some time and grew heated without reaching any conclusion.

'I think he's just a man who likes privacy and thought he would get it here,' was Helen's attitude.

'Anyway, there's no story at the present. We'll worry about whether I can use the material when I find something worth writing about,' Harry finally declared, and left after instructing them both to keep a close watch on Mr Bridges.

It took Helen a long time to get to sleep that night. The information about John, she could not think of him as David, inevitably altered the way she saw him.

Helen thumped her pillow angrily. At least Michelle must have been very upset indeed when she discovered that the man she had discarded as insufficiently wealthy had gone on to become a millionaire! How bitterly she must have regretted letting him see her true nature!

It did explain why she kept reappearing in his life, however. Even as merely the former Mrs Bridges, she probably felt entitled to some of his money.

7

The next morning, while she ironed busily, she was brooding on how she would react when she next met John Bridges. Would she be able to behave as if she still had no idea of his true identity? Mary interrupted her thoughts.

'Helen! Come here quickly!' she hissed from the terrace, beckoning urgently Helen unplugged the iron and hurried out, and Mary pointed down at the pavement. A taxi had drawn up and the driver was standing by the downstairs front door. John Bridges opened it, there was a brief conversation, and the driver stepped inside, reappearing shortly carrying two suitcases that he put in the boot of his taxi.

John Bridges soon followed him with another two cases. There was pause, and then Michelle sauntered into view. She was dressed in a smart linen suit topped with a matching wide-brimmed hat, an ensemble far more suited to a city than a seaside resort. When she reached the two men who stood waiting for her, she placed a hand on John's shoulder and kissed him on the cheek.

The driver sprang to open the taxi door, Michelle slid elegantly in, the driver closed the door, got into the driving seat, and the vehicle sped away while John Bridges gazed after it. Then he turned and looked up at the terrace, spotting Mary and Helen before they could draw back. Suddenly he smiled, waved at the energetically, and retreated into his apartment. They heard the door shut firmly.

'She's left him!' exclaimed Mary.

'Or he's thrown her out,' Helen said. 'Anyway, I'm glad she had gone. I didn't like her.'

Mary gave her a long look. 'You mean you do like John Bridges. What exactly did happen when you went to Barcelona? I thought your story was a little lacking in details.'

'Nothing happened,' Helen snapped, and went back to the ironing.

When she went down the next day to clean she was half-hoping that the apartment would be empty, but John Bridges emerged from a bedroom and greeted her cheerfully.

'You can strip the bed in there,' he indicated. 'As you saw yesterday, Michelle has left me yet again. Apparently she was invited to cruise the Mediterranean on a yacht and decided that was infinitely preferable to sharing a small apartment in Sitges with me.'

Helen nodded, avoided his eyes, and made for the kitchen. Some time later, as she was cleaning the sink, she realised that he was leaning against the doorframe, watching her.

'What's the matter, Helen?' he said. 'You are behaving as if I'd upset you somehow.'

'Nothing's the matter. I'm just in a hurry.'

He fell silent, but as she tried to

concentrate on her work she was conscious of him watching her. Suddenly she threw down the cloth and turned to face him.

'We know who you really are!' she announced. 'You are David Bridges, a rich businessman. Why are you staying in this little apartment?'

He folded his arms and grimaced resignedly. 'I suppose your journalist friend found out.' He moved forward, took her by the elbow and steered her into the living room. 'Sit down, and let me explain.'

She sat primly in the centre of the couch while he paced up and down.

'Did your friend happen to say how long I've been rich?'

She shook her head.

'Until just under two years ago I was getting on quite well. I was making enough money to be comfortable, and it looked as if that was how things would go on. Then a firm in which I'd invested a lot of time and most of my money went bust. One of the managers absconded with all the cash he could, confidence in the firm vanished, it shut down, and I found that I had very little money left.

'I wasn't prepared to spend another ten years just to get back where I'd been before, so I took a chance and invested every penny I could raise in a wildcat enterprise that everyone said was going to fail. They were wrong, and according to my accountant I am in fact now a millionaire. But I'm not used to being rich yet, and I don't spend money just because I can. I needed a place where I could get some work done, and I chose here. I could have rented a villa, but that would have come with a housekeeper, a cook, a gardener, etc. I just wanted somewhere quiet and comfortable where I could enjoy the sun when I wanted a break.' He stopped. 'You do understand, don't you?'

Helen nodded, and managed a smile.

'I suppose so. You are David Bridges, millionaire, but you still forget to buy fresh milk when you need it.'

'David is my first name and I use it in business, but my friends call me John. And I shall be most grateful if you will buy some more basics for me.'

'I'll do that later, John.' She was smiling naturally now. 'I'll get on with the cleaning. Michelle is not a tidy woman. Incidentally, did she find her book?'

'Her book?' John seemed taken aback and she explained that she had found Michelle hunting for a missing book. He raised his eyebrows, and then understanding showed in his eyes and he grinned slowly. 'No, I don't think she found what she was looking for.'

Days later Helen was reflecting on how quickly things could change. Only recently all she wanted was a quiet, trouble-free family in the downstairs apartment and a peaceful life for herself with Mary and the children. Now she was living above a mysterious million-aire and Mary was often missing, out with Harry Lyne. Quite often during the day she didn't even want Helen to take care of the children.

'If Harry wants to play a part in my life then he's going to have to accept that they come with me,' she said firmly, and so far he seemed perfectly happy to do just that. Harry, Mary and the children played on the beach, swam in the sea, went shopping together, just like a normal family, and more and more often Harry was there for lunch and the evening meal.

'As soon as I go back to England you will be able to spend every evening together,' Helen said.

'Here in the apartment. But without you to babysit it will mean goodbye to candlelit dinners in restaurants!' Mary hugged Helen. 'Anyway,' she pointed out, 'if it hadn't been for you I would never have met him.'

An unexpected solution to the problem appeared one morning. Helen was by herself, wondering whether it was worth the bother or making one cup of coffee, when there was firm knock on the door and she opened it to find John Bridges outside. She had not seen him for a few days and was surprised how glad she was to find him at the door.

'Come in!' she said warmly. 'You can be my excuse to make some coffee.'

After a few minutes' bustle they were seated on the terrace with the coffee tray between them.

'Can I help you? Is everything all right?' Helen asked her unexpected guest.

'Everything in the apartment is fine. I shall be quite sorry to leave it.'

Helen felt shocked. She had lost track of his tenancy. Of course, he would be leaving soon!

'Well, I'm glad you have enjoyed your stay. Perhaps you can recommend us to some other millionaires.'

'Or perhaps I'll come back next year. No, I'm not here to complain. I had another reason for wanting to see you.' He fell silent, frowning, and she waited patiently till he looked up with sudden determination. 'The thing is, I've got to go to Barcelona again and I'll be away overnight.'

'That's no problem,' Helen assured him. 'Just tell me the date and I'll tell Mary.'

'I'm going tomorrow,' he informed her, and then looked at her impatiently. 'The date's not impor- tant. The reason I'm telling you is that — I'd like you to come with me!' he finished in a rush.

Helen gaped at him inelegantly. 'What do you mean?'

John took a deep breath. 'I mean that I am going to Barcelona for a meeting tomorrow afternoon, and then I've got to stay over for a night. That means I'll have plenty of time to explore Barce- lona but I don't want to do it on my own.' He finished in a rush, and looked at her expectantly.

Helen was gazing at him wide-eyed, completely taken aback. It was true that they had achieved a mildly friendly relationship but what exactly was he proposing now?

'You mean,' she said slowly, 'that we go to Barcelona tomorrow, then you go to your meeting, but when you are free we look round the city together.'

He nodded. 'But why me?' she asked. 'You obviously know people in Barcelona. Surely one of them would be willing to accompany you.'

He poured himself another cup of coffee without being asked. 'The people in Barcelona are purely business acquaintances. Anyway, I thought of you because I know how much you want to see more of Barcelona. And I'm not blind. I see who comes in and out here and I know your journalist friend takes your friend, Mary, out quite a lot nowadays. If you come with me, it will give the pair of them a chance to spend some time together here without you.'

Helen was hesitating. Some things were still not clear. 'I'll have to see if the hotel in Barcelona has a room free.'

John shrugged impatiently. 'You can forget that tourist dump. There are some advantages to being rich. I have already booked accommodation at a good hotel in Barcelona, and I do not intend to waste time going from my hotel to pick you up at yours.'

Helen thought fast.

'One room or two?' she asked bluntly.

He gave her a startled look and then guffawed with laughter. 'Don't worry, Miss Corby, I have no evil designs on your honour. Two rooms.'

She was conscious of relief as well as a very faint pang of wounded pride. It was rather too obvious that he had indeed only thought of her as a sightseeing companion. She drew herself up.

'I can't afford a luxury hotel and I can't let you pay for me!'

'Of course you can! I'm rich, and you have to spend your time cleaning and child minding to get a holiday in Spain. Give me a chance to spend a bit of my money. Look at it as a thank you, a tip for your services.'

'That usually means a box of chocolate.'

It was a very tempting offer, however, Helen brooded while John Bridges watched her.

'As you say, it would give Mary time to be here with Harry without having to worry about me,' she said slowly.

He nodded firmly. 'It would be unkind of you not to give them the opportunity.'

'And you are right — I would love to see more of Barcelona.'

'And you would see it in comfort. You would stay at a good hotel and eat at good restaurants, and I promise you I would be an excellent guide.'

She made up her mind. 'Well, then, for Mary's sake, and to stop you being lonely, I'll come!'

He raised his cup of coffee in a mock toast. 'I will try to see that your self-sacrifice is rewarded. We'll catch the two o'clock train tomorrow and make sure you pack everything in one bag!'

Mary's reaction to the news when she returned was mixed.

'Are you sure, Helen? It sounds very odd.'

'I know. But I do believe him. I think he is trying to make up for his bad temper when he first came here and he was under stress for some reason. Anyway, if he does turn out to have wicked plans, or wants more in the way of gratitude than a thank-you, I'm a big, tough girl.'

'Very well, then.' Mary's eyes had a faraway look and Helen wondered whether she was already planning what to serve Harry for a quiet dinner in the apartment.

Harry was busy elsewhere that evening, attending a conference which he expected to yield a few saleable paragraphs for the business press, and after Peter and Shula had been put to bed, Helen started to pack. For one night away, she would usually have got everything into one small holdall, but this time, with visions of an expensive hotel and dinner in a good restaurant, the pile of clothes she thought essential grew bigger and bigger.

'I don't know what I'll need,' she complained. 'Suppose it's the kind of restaurant where people wear evening dresses. Do I need a dressing gown?'

Mary went through the pile ruthlessly.

'You can take that pretty sundress you've hardly worn. That will do any restaurant. You only need one pair of sandals you can walk in and some comfortable shoes,' she added, removing the high-heeled evening shoes which Helen had bought in a fit of extravagance, only to find that they were very uncomfortable to wear. 'Just remember, you are going to sightsee, not attend some grand social event.'

Finally the remaining clothes were safely stowed in the usual holdall and Helen went to bed exhausted and slept soundly.

John called for her just as lunch was being cleared away, and Helen was horrified to see that he was wearing the formal suit in which she had first seen him. He carried a briefcase as well as a small holdall, and was clutching a small packet.

'I haven't packed any smart clothes!' she said, wondering how long it would take her to repack her bag.

'Good! This suit is for the meeting, and as soon as it is finished I shall be changing into my jeans,' he informed her, 'Now, I wondered if your friend would do me a favour.' He held out the packet. 'I bought some steak and I'm not sure it will keep fresh in the refrigerator. Would your friend mind putting it in her freezer? I assume she has one.'

Helen tucked the packet into the freezer and then the couple set out.

The train to Barcelona was, as usual, full of tourists going to enjoy its sights and Spaniards planning to enjoy its shops, and there was no need to make conversation on the short journey. When they left the train and surfaced in the middle of the city, John instantly flagged down a taxi to take them to the hotel.

It was, indeed, very different from Helen's previous hotel. It was very impressive indeed, an obviously merited the five stars which it displayed discreetly. The décor was charming and welcoming, and the hotel was in an ideal position to explore Barcelona, situated between the Gothic Quarter and the nineteenth-century area of the city.

As John took care of checking-in details, Helen was relieved of her bag by a polite young man who guided her to her room, put down the bag, and vanished before she could wonder whether he would expect a tip or not, leaving her to explore a bedroom whose floor area was nearly as large as that of Mary's whole apartment. It was very comfortable. In fact she decided that it was the first hotel she had ever stayed in that justified the word 'luxurious'.

When she opened the door in

response to a quiet knock, John was outside.

'I am in the next room, but I'm afraid I have got to go now,' he told her. 'If you want anything to eat or drink, order it from room service. I hope I won't be too late back.'

'Don't worry. I'll be happy just walking around the streets for an hour or so — and I'll watch the traffic.'

It was a fascinating afternoon as she wandered from elegant nineteenth-century streets into the ancient heart of the city, down to the sea, and then on to the striking modern buildings with which Barcelona had transformed its seafront when it staged the Olympic Games. Helen visited an impressive aquarium and followed the tunnels of glass that let her see a shark swimming lazily above her. Later pleasantly tired, she sipped a glass of white wine in the Plaza Real.

Back at the hotel, Reception informed her that Mr Bridges had not yet returned. She decided to have a shower to freshen up for the evening, then looked at the enormous bathtub and resolved to wallow in that instead. A range of toiletries waited for her, and her eyes widened as she recognised the name of a very expensive brand. She slipped a small bottle of shampoo and guest soap in her toilet bag. Mary would appreciate those!

She lay soaking for some time in the scented bubbles and was drifting into a doze when she heard a knock. Hastily she got out of the bath and wrapped herself in the towelling robe provided.

'I'm sorry. I didn't realise how time was passing,' she apologised, but John seemed unconcerned.

'I just came to tell you that I'm back. A shower seems a good idea,' he said, and she was aware of his eyes lazily scanning her. She realised the robe was very loosely wrapped around her, and hastily pulled it tighter, but John didn't seem to notice.

'I'll see you in about half-an-hour,' he informed her, turning away towards his own room.

Helen spent the time preparing for the evening out as best she could. The sundress did suit her, emphasising her slim waist with its full skirt, and her scanty supply of cosmetics enabled her to emphasise her eyes and lips. When John reappeared she was relieved to see that he was casually dressed in jeans and a T-shirt with a loose linen jacket. He lifted his eyebrows and gave an approving nod as he looked at her.

'I can just fade into the background this evening. All eyes will be on you,' he commented.

Helen felt herself blushing. 'At least I look better than I do when I'm cleaning your bathroom.'

He gave a sudden grin that made him look much younger. 'You do indeed. Now let's go and enjoy ourselves.'

Helen had thought Barcelona was busy in the afternoon as the tourists thronged the streets, but now as dusk fell the people of Barcelona themselves had come out for the evening, and Helen hesitated at the sight of the crowds.

'Come this way,' John said, seizing her hand, and led her down narrow side streets and alleyways till they found themselves in a quiet corner where a few tables had been placed outside a bar.

'What would you like? Red wine, white wine, a beer?'

'I thought we were going to have dinner,' she commented, uneasily aware that her stomach was telling her urgently that she had not eaten since lunch with Mary and the children.

John looked shocked. 'It's barely seven o'clock. I told you the last time we were here, Barcelona starts eating about nine or ten.'

'Then I'll have a white wine,' she decided, but when the wine arrived she was relieved to see that it was accompanied by little dishes of olives, tiny fried fish and prawns sizzling in garlic, together with some bread.

They shared the savoury morsels, dipping bread into the delicious oil left on the plates.

'Have you been to this bar before?' she asked, hoping he had not noticed how swiftly she had seized the last prawn.

'Several times,' he told her, and beckoned to the waiter. A minute later, a fresh plate of prawns appeared. 'A lot of my business is with Spanish firms, but the first time I came here I was young and inexperienced and I shall always be grateful to the man who took pity and showed me the real Barcelona.'

'Who was he?'

'Someone whose firm was having trouble a few years later because bigger firms were trying to put him out of business. I was able to help him, to our mutual benefit.'

He saw her looking at him.

'What is it?'

She carefully peeled another prawn. 'I'm still trying to see you as a very rich man, a power player in business.'

He sipped his wine. 'People play games — in the playground, at work in their private lives. I just play games on a bigger scale, that's all. I guess what people are going to do and see what manoeuvres I can carry out.'

'And do you enjoy doing that?'

'Yes,' he said without hesitation. 'Some people play computer games. I'm using my brain and my skills against real people. It's more fun.'

8

Afterwards they wandered back to the busy streets. At one point John took hold of her hand as they were nearly swept apart by a group of tourists, and somehow he kept his grip on her even when they could move more freely.

'You don't have to follow the tourist route,' he said, waving his free hand at the colourful crowd. 'The whole city is one big spectacle.'

They meandered down Las Ramblas and found themselves by the massive column on which stood Christopher Columbus, proudly pointing out to sea, but, as Helen quickly pointed out, in the opposite direction to America.

'Don't be so fussy,' John reproved her. 'You couldn't have him pointing up a shopping street!'

Helen's head was still tipped back,

gazing up at the dark figure outlined against the sky.

'At least he had a dream, and he followed it. I envy him. So far I have gone through life doing what seemed the sensible thing. Soon I'll be going back to teacher training. My life seems very predictable, and rather dull.'

He laughed softly. 'Helen Corby, may I point out that you are in one of the most exciting cities in the world, and you are with a wealthy young man who is about to take you for a very good meal. Forget the future and enjoy tonight.'

She blinked. 'I am enjoying tonight — very much. I'm just afraid that after this everything will be an anticlimax.'

'Only if you let it be. Find your dream, like Columbus, and follow it.'

Slowly she smiled. 'Well, at the moment I am dreaming of that good meal. I am hungry.'

'Fortunately the restaurant is not far from here.'

The restaurant was not grand, its

décor was not the work of some highly-paid designer, but the service and the food were impeccable. At the end Helen gave a contented sigh.

'Now every meal I have will be measured against this!'

John beckoned the waiter. 'I could tell from the amount you ate that you approved.' He held up a hand hastily. 'And I admit I ate at least as much. Now, I suggest we go back to the Plaza Real for a coffee and a brandy.'

It was after midnight when they finally returned to the hotel. Helen opened her door and turned to say goodnight to John.

'It has been a perfect evening,' she said softly.

He brushed a strand of hair away from her cheek and looked down at her wordlessly. She lifted her face to his and waited for his kiss, but it did not come, and after a moment he stepped away from her.

'A kiss would not be enough,' he said. 'And gratitude is not a good enough reason. Goodnight, Helen.'

He turned and left her.

When she woke up the next morning Helen was horrified to see that it was nearly nine o'clock. She scrambled out of bed and made for the bathroom, wondering when was she supposed to meet John. Just as important, where could she get breakfast?

She emerged from a quick shower to the smell of coffee and found a generous breakfast tray waiting on the bedroom table. Half an hour later, when she had eaten and dressed, John telephoned.

'I'll meet you in Reception in ten minutes.'

In jeans and sweatshirt, he looked out of place in the stately surroundings of the hotel's entrance hall, but the smiles that greeted him and the speed with which the doorman sprang to open the door for them showed the hotel saw him as a valued guest.

'Now we are not going to go on the tourist bus or follow a prescribed route,' he told Helen firmly. 'We are just going to see what we can find.'

The next few hours were a kaleidoscope of sights and sounds. At one time Helen was staring up at great grey stone knights, at another she was looking at broken Roman columns, then a vegetable market full of colour and haggling housewives. Children played on a concrete mammoth, and fountains played in front of palaces.

Finally they sank down gratefully at a kiosk in a park and John ordered sandwiches and beer.

'This is marvellous,' Helen said gratefully, turning her face up to the sun.

'You've enjoyed the morning?'

'I've loved every minute!'

He gave her a long look. 'I believe you have. And so have I.'

The food and beer arrived and they welcomed them eagerly.

'Did you ever come here with Michelle?' Helen asked, remembering the elegance of his former wife.

John, his mouth full of bread and ham, shook his head forcefully.

'I certainly did not!' he said when he could speak. 'Michelle believed in luxury, not a snack in the park. I didn't show her round Barcelona, either. Michelle wasn't interested in anything but herself.' He looked at Helen questioningly. 'What about that boyfriend you told me about, the idiot who dumped you?'

Helen shrugged. 'He would have conscientiously gone round every sight, guide book in hand. He liked everything to be organised. I think he got together with me because he thought I was like that, but I'm beginning to find that I like a little unexpected excitement.'

John looked sideways at her. 'Are you sure that everything is over between you, that he won't come back?'

Helen drank some beer thoughtfully. 'I think so. He made it pretty clear that he didn't feel the same way about me as I thought I did about him.'

'Suppose he did reappear, would you welcome that?'

She shrugged impatiently, a little annoyed at his persistence.

'There's no use speculating. It's not likely to happen.' She sat up. 'When do we have to leave the hotel?'

He accepted the change of subject. 'We can leave it for a few hours, but perhaps we had better go back soon. I told Mary I would have you back in Sitges by early evening, if that is all right with you.'

'That's fine. Anyway, my feet are beginning to feel a little bit tired.'

Back at the hotel, it took Helen five minutes to pack her bag. She stood for a moment before she left the room, looking round and carefully memorising every detail so that she would be able to tell Mary all about it. She doubted if she would ever stay in such luxury again.

The train journey back to Sitges was uneventful. When they reached Mary's building everything was quiet, all the windows shut.

'Mary must have gone shopping or to the beach with the children,' Helen guessed. 'I'll unpack and wait for her.'

'Why not wait downstairs with me?' John said unexpectedly. 'I've enjoyed your company, Helen, and I'm not eager to see the back of you. Come and have a coffee.'

It was growing dark now, and coffee with John would be better than waiting alone upstairs, Helen persuaded herself, as John unlocked the door and she followed him in. But as he fumbled for the light switch footsteps rushed towards them, a hand was pressed across her mouth while her arms were pulled behind her, and she was bundled towards the living room and thrust down on the couch while sounds told her that the same thing was happening to John. Then a torch beam cut through the darkness, focussing on the two of them. Helen pulled herself upright.

'What are you doing?' she demanded. 'This is a holiday apartment. There's nothing worth stealing here.'

'Mr Bridges knows better.'

The language was English but with a Spanish accent and now Helen could make out three men facing them. One she recognised as the intruder she had driven out days earlier.

John thrust aside the hand that was still trying to gag him.

'She's right. There's nothing here,' John said coldly.

'I don't believe you,' the man said flatly.

'I think he's speaking the truth. I can't find anything anywhere.'

This was a new voice, a woman's voice, and as the torch beam swung towards the doorway another figure appeared.

'Michelle!' Helen cried out in amazement. John regarded his former wife with disgust.

'I should have guessed why you suddenly appeared at that particular time,' he said. 'Well, you are wasting your efforts. The information isn't here.'

The man shrugged. 'We know you have deleted the files from your computer, but you wouldn't have done that without making a copy. If all else fails, well, I'm sure you can remember a considerable amount, and I am confident we can persuade you to talk, especially if you know we will harm this young lady if you don't.'

Helen stared at him in horrified disbelief. What did he want so much that he was prepared to threaten her? She was turning towards John when she became aware of noises outside the window. She could hear the high, childish voices of Peter and Shula. Mary and the children must be coming back, and she had to warn them before they were seized as well, but as she opened her mouth to scream a warning hand was clapped over her mouth again and the torch was switched off. But a hand was free!

She reached towards the coffee table at the end of the couch, felt for a stone ornament which she knew stood on it, and hurled it towards the window. There was a satisfying crash of glass, and though the iron grille stopped the ornament going any further there was also a loud thud, perfectly audible from outside. The children's voices stopped suddenly.

'What's going on? Who's there?' she heard Harry Lyne exclaim. 'Mary, take the children away. I'm going to find out who's in there!'

Then there was another crash as Harry burst through the front door and launched himself into the living room. The next minute was full of confused activity. As Harry tackled one man, John hurled himself off the couch at another. Not to be left out, Helen was hitting and kicking the third in a very unladylike manner, dimly conscious of Michelle running out of the house. That was a pity! She would have liked to tackle that lady!

The intruders might threaten a helpless woman but they were not fighters. As soon as they could evade their attackers they fled, the sound of their running steps soon lost in the tangled streets of the old town.

'We'll never be able to follow them now,' Harry complained.

There was a horrified exclamation. Mary had seen the men run away and had decided it was safe to venture back and she had switched the lights on. With the children clinging nervously to her, she gazed around the wrecked apartment. It was now possible to see the mess that the intruders had made during their search. Jars and packets of food had been emptied on to the kitchen floor and upholstery had been slashed to see if anything had been concealed in seating or beds.

John had taken Helen in his arms.

'Did they hurt you?'

She shook her head. 'A couple of bumps, that's all. I hope I hurt one of them, though.'

'I'll call the police,' Harry said grimly, taking out his mobile phone, but John shook his head urgently.

'No! There's no need for that. I'll pay for everything to be repaired or replaced.'

The two men stared at each other.

'If you're not willing to call the police it must be because you are involved with something illegal,' declared white-faced Mary, but John shook his head vehemently.

'Honestly, I'm not. But what I would have to tell the police could cause more trouble than it's worth.'

'You can't leave it at that. You owe us an explanation,' Harry exclaimed.

'I know.' John dabbed his cheek, where blood was trickling down after the fight. 'Give me half-an-hour.'

Harry made a quick decision, sliding his mobile back in his pocket.

'You can have an hour. That will give us time to get the children to bed. Then you can come upstairs and tell us everything. And don't think you can sneak away, because I'll be watching. Come on, Mary.'

Upstairs the children were reassured

that everything was all right and that the nasty men had gone for good.

John appeared punctually on the hour and Harry took him out on the terrace where Helen and Mary were waiting. When John had asked how Helen was, and the ritual of offering and drinking coffee had been gone through, Harry put his cup down firmly and leant forward.

'We are listening, Mr Bridges.' When John appeared to hesitate, Harry frowned blackly. 'You can't go back on your word now.'

'I don't intend to!' John flung back indignantly. 'It's just that it is rather hard to explain. It is to do with business — high finance.'

'We'll tell you when we can't follow.'

John sat back. 'It is all to do with two firms — two very big, multinational firms. For various reasons, they have decided to merge, and I have been working out many of the details. Those men — and Michelle — wanted that information.'

Helen waited, but he did not go on.

'Is that all?' she asked incredulously, but Harry was nodding comprehension.

'Information about a big merger is valuable, Helen. It gives people an opportunity to buy shares before the price goes up, to sell information to rival firms so that they can try to complicate matters. Advance information about a really big merger could be worth millions.'

'And if the information is made public too soon it can cause damage. Markets become uncertain, employees start wondering about their jobs, nobody wants to take any decisions until they know what is happening,' John added. 'All we need is silence for another week, then everything will be made public and there won't be any uncertainty.'

'What firms are we talking about?' asked Harry, and when John did not answer he shook his head. 'I'm a journalist, Mr Bridges. I can find out whom you have been working with recently. This could be a big break for me. What can you offer in return for my silence?'

John looked at him directly.

'You saved Helen and me this evening. I am in your debt. I am prepared to give you the press release twenty-four hours before it goes out to everyone else, and I'll give you a few extra facts, a few stories, as well. You can have your story written in advance by the release date and sell it worldwide.'

Harry was smiling. 'I accept. Just one thing more.'

'What?'

'I want an interview with you.'

'I don't give interviews.'

'That's why one would be so valuable.' He glanced at Mary. 'I want the money, Mr Bridges. I expect to be taking on new responsibilities soon.'

Helen saw Mary's cheeks flame scarlet as John nodded.

'Then I agree. You can have your interview.'

Harry grinned and sat back, but

seconds later he was sitting up and frowning again.

'But there is one thing I don't understand. Helen told me what happened, and I agree with those men. You may have sent or taken the details of the merger plans elsewhere, but you would have kept a copy. They looked very thoroughly and didn't find it. Where is it?'

John's broad smile was definitely tinged with smugness. 'Not far.'

'Where?'

John turned to Helen. 'Do you remember the steak I asked you to put in Mary's freezer?'

She nodded slowly.

'Well, there's a computer disc in between the steaks.'

They absorbed this information in silence.

'Are you afraid those men might return?' Mary asked tentatively.

'No. They aren't violent types. They only talked tough today because they saw it as their last chance after Michelle had tried to get the information out of me first and then they searched the place and found nothing. I'm sure they will decide to cut their losses. I'll be all right.'

Soon afterwards he stood up, yawning.

'One way or another, it's been a full day. Time for bed. Incidentally, I'll take the steak and disc with me now.' He grinned as Harry's face fell. 'Did you think I'd forget that?'

Helen saw him to the stairs. Out of sight of the other two, he took her hand.

'I am so sorry you got involved in the trouble earlier. Are you sure you are all right, Helen?'

'Just one or two tender spots. I only wish I could have got my hands on Michelle.'

He laughed softly. 'She has lost, and at least I've got something out of this sorry mess. She'll never dare come near me again!'

Harry was full of excitement at what he obviously saw as a major coup in his career as a journalist, and did his best to convince the girls that it was perfectly possible to work out the most intricate business matters with a computer and internet access. He left late and it was the following morning before Helen and Mary could have a private conversation over their recent experiences.

Helen assured Mary that she had had a wonderful time in Barcelona and told her all about the hotel and the restaurant.

'John Bridges was a very good companion, but that was all,' she told her friend, deciding to ignore that moment outside her hotel room.

'That is a pity. When else are you likely to meet a young, presentable millionaire?'

'Oh, there will be plenty at teaching college, I'm sure! What about you? I gather Harry wants something more than companionship?'

A gentle smile curved Mary's lips. 'Oh, yes! We talked and talked last night, and we've decided we want to be together. It will be perfect. The children will have a new father and I'll have a live-in handyman, while Harry will have someone to do his ironing.' She saw the look of incredulity on Helen's face and burst out laughing. 'I'm teasing you, Helen! We love each other!'

'Then both of you have my congratulations and best wishes!' Helen exclaimed and embraced her friend. A thought struck her. 'Aren't you lucky? Your parents definitely approved of him!'

Harry appeared briefly before spending a couple of hours with John Bridges. Afterwards he looked very satisfied and told Helen and Mary that he thought the interview had gone well. He could not stay longer, as he had to go away for the night to cover a festival in Tarragona, so the girls spent a quiet evening together.

Mary was lost in her own thoughts, obviously dreaming happily of a life with Harry Lyne. Helen watched her enviously before brooding on her own future.

9

Helen and Mary had done the best they could to tidy and clean the downstairs apartment and John escorted Mary and Helen to a furniture shop where he paid for new beds and a suite. The shop promised the goods would be delivered within the week.

'So they will be here for the next tenants,' Mary said with pleasure.

'They may even be here before I leave on Saturday,' John remarked, and Helen gave him a startled glance. Just two more days and he would be gone.

'I have to be in London when the news about the merger breaks,' he told her. She understood but it was still a shock. Over the summer she had become accustomed to getting to know Mary's tenants, only to forget about them when they left and a new group arrived. But John had been here longer than any and their shared experiences had made her think of him as a friend.

Now she had to remind herself of how little time they had in fact spent together and told herself that once he had returned to London and was caught up again in the world of high finance he would soon forget the girl who had cleaned the apartment and given him someone to talk to as he went round Barcelona.

Already as they walked back to the apartments together, his mind seemed to be on other matters. He thanked them for the clean rooms and assured Mary that he could sleep perfectly well on his ruined bed till the new ones arrived.

When Helen next clattered down the steps early with her bucket and cleaning tools, it was only to find that John had already gone out. Impatiently she carried out the few necessary tasks. A knock on the door turned out to be a delivery man with the new furniture, so she called Mary down to supervise its installation. When it was satisfactorily in place and the ruined furniture removed, Mary stood back with her hands on her hips, looked round the living room, and gave a sigh of relief.

'Well, it looks as if that episode is over. The Thomson family will be coming in a few days and then we shall be back to normal.'

She went back to Peter and Shula while Helen put bedclothes on the new beds. As she was closing the front door behind her, she saw John walking towards the house, and waited to greet him.

'The new furniture has arrived and the apartment looks good. It's a pity you won't have long to enjoy it.'

'I'm just glad it arrived in time to avoid problems with the new tenants.'

He hesitated. 'Helen, tonight is my last night in Sitges. I was wondering whether you would come out to dinner with me.'

Helen was conscious of a warm glow in her cheeks and a pleasant flutter, but before she could accept the invitation they were interrupted. A taxi drew up beside them as they stood together on the pavement and a tall figure erupted from it.

'Helen!' she heard, and was instantly enveloped in the newcomer's strong arms. She struggled to loosen his grasp and found herself looking up into a familiar face that she had never expected to see in Spain.

'George!' she exclaimed. 'What are you doing here?'

Her former boyfriend smiled down at her possessively. 'I'm here to see you, of course, to tell you how much I love you.'

It was not only unexpected, it was highly embarrassing. Helen wriggled free. Looking round desperately, she saw that John had vanished and heard his door shut emphatically. She turned back to George.

'You'd better come upstairs and explain.'

George paid the taxi driver, reclaimed

a bag, and followed Helen.

'George has arrived,' Helen announced loudly as Mary and her children appeared. Mary greeted him coolly, aware of how much he had hurt Helen, and Peter and Shula sensed her mood and hid behind her, but George did not seem to realise how lukewarm his reception was.

'It's great to see you,' he told Mary, planting a smacking kiss on her forehead. 'Your mother told me you were doing well.'

Mary and Helen exchanged looks. He had given them a vital clue. Somehow Mrs Loughborough was responsible for his arrival.

'Where are you staying?' Mary asked, pointedly ignoring the bag he had dumped on the floor. George smiled ingratiatingly.

'I booked a flight at the last minute, so I haven't reserved a room anywhere. Haven't you got a couch I could sleep on?'

Helen needed to talk to him, and she couldn't do that at the apartment with

Mary and the children within earshot.

'George, why don't you and I go down to the beach? We can call in for a drink somewhere and catch up with things.'

Even George could not ignore the implicit command in her tone, and soon they were strolling towards the seafront. George tried to take her hand but she snatched it away. They found a small table outside a bar and ordered beers. As he took his first long swallow she eyed him critically, noticing for the first time how his coarse yellow curls were already thinning at the front.

'This is a great place,' he commented, glancing round at the view. 'You did the right thing coming here.'

'I came here to get over the fact that you had told me you were in love with someone else and wouldn't be seeing me again,' she said crisply. 'Now you appear without warning, claiming that you love me after all. What has happened, George?'

He smiled at her and reached across

the table to hold her hand. 'Mrs Loughborough called me. She told me how lonely you were, how much you were missing me, and I realised what a fool I'd been and how much I loved you and I came here to tell you so as soon as I could.'

So this was the 'favour' Mrs Loughborough had mentioned! She drew her hand away.

'And what about that other girl you said you loved?'

He shrugged uneasily, a frown hovering. Obviously she was supposed to be so overcome with gratitude by his sudden reappearance and protestations of love that she forgot the past.

'I realised I'd made a mistake.'

'Or she realised she'd made one, and you thought you would soothe your bruised ego by giving me a second chance.' Helen sat up straight. 'Listen, George. I thought I loved you once, but fortunately you told me it was all over between us. I came here to get over you, and I have. Mrs Loughborough

164

was wrong. I don't love you. In fact I don't even like you. So you can go off somewhere else for a holiday or you can go straight home, but I don't want you hanging round here.'

He gaped at her, then shook his head and laughed. 'I hurt you, and you are trying to get your revenge. Helen, don't be bitter. We should be thinking about the future, not the past.'

'I am, and it doesn't include you.' She stood up. 'Now, pay the man for the beers.'

Upset, completely disconcerted, he paid reluctantly. Helen watched him carefully counting out the coins, remembering his meanness in little things. She started walking back to the apartment so rapidly that he found it difficult to keep pace with her.

'But what am I going to do? Where am I going to stay?' he complained.

'There are plenty of hotels in the area. Find one.'

He halted and she turned to face him. 'Helen, don't be silly. I've come all this way, paid for my flight, you can't just send me away!'

'Yes, I can!' she said. 'What do you expect me to do? Refund your fare? I didn't want you to come here and I don't want you to stay.'

She stalked on ahead of him.

'George is leaving — now,' she informed Mary, picking up George's bag and handing it to him. 'Will you call him a taxi?'

'There's no need. I'll walk to the station,' George said with wounded dignity as he took the bag. 'Goodbye, Mary. I shall be speaking to your mother about this.'

Then he was gone, leaving Mary staring at Helen.

'Tell me what happened,' she ordered, and Helen did.

'So he's gone, and I'm glad,' she finished. 'Now, I've just got to go and have a word with John.'

'But you can't! He's gone too! A few minutes after you went out with George, John Bridges came upstairs and said that he had changed his mind and decided to leave today. He said there was nothing to keep him here and he could get on with work better back in London. I called a taxi and he left just before you got back.'

Helen bit her lip and sat down. So there would be no farewell dinner with John Bridges. Well, she had known he was going. It would have been nice to say goodbye, but did it really matter? She forced a smile.

'Open a bottle of wine, Mary. Let's toast the end of an episode.'

Harry appeared that evening and Mary told him the whole story. 'I knew Bridges had gone. He sent me an email telling me exactly when to expect the press release, and I'm not sorry I've missed George. He sounds a real pain.'

'At least I am absolutely sure now that I don't love him any longer. In fact, I don't think I ever did.' Helen drew a deep breath. 'I've been thinking since he went, and I've come to a big decision. I'm not going to train as a teacher.' They looked startled and she went on to explain. 'I realised I was only drifting into teaching because I couldn't think of anything else to do, and the children deserve better than that.'

'What are you going to do instead?' Mary asked.

'I'm not sure yet. I'll get temporary jobs, widen my experience, and then maybe I'll find my dream. I would like to write children's stories. Peter and Shula like the ones I've made up and told them.'

Mary looked uncertain but Harry was nodding approvingly.

'You are doing the right thing. Find your dream and follow it, though it may not work out just as you expected. Mine didn't, but I enjoy journalism and odd-jobbing, and I earn enough to marry the woman I love and get a ready-made family.' He raised his glass in a toast. 'Here's to a new future for all of us!'

The next day Helen informed the

college by email that she was withdrawing from the teacher training course 'for personal reasons' and Mary asked her to stay in Sitges till the end of the season.

'I've come to rely on your help with the apartment, and Harry and I are planning to get married in early October so I would like you to be here for that.'

Helen agreed to stay with relief. She would have a few more weeks to think about what she would do when she returned to England.

There was an awkward ten minutes when Mrs Loughborough, back from England, telephoned to say how upset she was at the way poor George had been treated, but Mary was unexpectedly firm and made it quite clear what she thought of George.

After waiting anxiously to see if John Bridges would keep his part of the bargain, Harry received the information about the big merger. Armed with his exclusive interview with John Bridges, he contacted various important papers and managed to arrange some profitable deals.

'At least the papers know I exist now, so they may contact me in the future, and the money I will get for the interview will practically pay for the swimming pool. It will be ready for the first visitors next year.'

The sun was still warm, but the autumnal days were growing shorter. Finally Mary and Helen waved the last guests farewell. Soon it would be Mary's wedding day. They had planned a quiet affair, with just a few friends and family. It had been agreed that the Loughboroughs would stay in the downstairs apartment for a couple of days before the wedding, and would then move upstairs to look after Peter and Shula while Mary and Harry went off for a honeymoon in the south of Spain. Helen planned to fly back to England the day after the wedding.

Helen had been worried that Mary's mother would still be annoyed with her about the George affair, but when she arrived Mrs Loughborough was obviously not interested in anything but her daughter's wedding. She kissed Helen on the cheek, announced that she just couldn't understand young girls nowadays, and never referred to the matter again.

Everybody agreed that it was a beautiful wedding. Mary wore a full-length dress of heavy cream silk. Designed with simple, flowing lines, the beauty of the fabric was enhanced by the bodice, embroidered with the same colour. Harry not only appeared in a suit for the very first time that anybody could remember, but managed to look very elegant in it. Shula revelled in her fairy-tale dress as a bridesmaid though Peter was less pleased by his pageboy's suit.

Helen, as chief bridesmaid, had no trouble controlling them, though she might have been helped by their awareness that Mrs Loughborough was keeping a close eye on their behaviour.

Helen saw the love in Harry's eyes as Mary came to stand beside him, and wondered whether any man would ever look at her in the same way.

The reception was held in a nearby hotel, and here not only the wedding guests but many other friends and neighbours wished the couple well. It was obvious that they were liked and accepted in Sitges by Spanish and British alike. Eventually everyone crowded on the pavement to wave Mary and Harry off as they took a taxi to Barcelona Airport, and later Helen and the Loughboroughs took the tired children home.

'It was a perfect day,' Mrs Loughborough said, misty-eyed. 'I know they will be very happy.' A touch of her usual sharp expression returned as she looked at Helen. 'Have you got everything ready, Helen? What are you going to do when you get back to England?'

Helen, back in jeans and a T-shirt, nodded.

'My suitcase is packed, so all I've got

to do in the morning is put a few things in my shoulder-bag. As for what I'm going to do when I get back, I'm going to stay with a friend in London for a few days so that I can look around and see what work is available. Then I shall go and see my parents.'

'How did they react when you told them you weren't going to be a teacher after all?'

'They didn't seem very surprised. My mother said I should do something I really wanted to do.'

'Only you don't know yet what you want to do.'

'I'll find out eventually.' She stood up. 'I think I'd better go to bed now. Today has been a long day, and tomorrow will be tiring as well.'

Helen went to sleep quickly but woke early to the realisation that this would be her last morning in Spain. Of course she would come here again, but as a visitor, and that would not be the same at all. Quickly she showered and slipped on the clothes she would wear to travel in, then added a light jacket and crept down the stairs into the quiet early morning.

She made her way to the promenade and stood for some time watching daylight spread across the sea. Helen remembered her first meeting with Harry Lyne, which had led to yesterday's wedding. She smiled as she thought of the scene which had taken place a few yards away when she had dismissed George. Then her face grew serious again as she recalled her conversation here with John, and that led to other memories of their brief acquaintanceship. She still wondered what they would have talked about if he had brought her here for a last dinner, and still regretted that she had not been able to say goodbye to him.

10

Helen had not booked a seat on a plane in advance because she had not been sure exactly what time she would be able to leave Sitges. After all, there were several flights a day from Barcelona to London and at that time of the year there were sure to be empty seats. In fact she was delayed for some time. Peter and Shula were reacting to the excitement of the previous day and were noisy and demanding, confident that they could take advantage of their doting grandparents, and it took Helen quite a time to steer them back to their normal behaviour.

She also had to convince Mr Loughborough that she really did not need to be driven to the airport, that he should stay and help his wife look after the twins. Then Mrs Loughborough insisted that Helen should have something to eat before she left and afterwards there were sticky farewell kisses and hugs from the twins. Finally, as she seized her bags and clattered down the stairs she found that Mrs Loughborough had followed her.

'I haven't been able to have a quiet word with you before, what with all the preparations for the wedding,' the older woman said with unaccustomed awkwardness. 'It's just that I wanted to thank you for all you have done for Mary. I don't know how she would have coped with these first few months here without your help.'

'Mary helped me as well,' Helen protested.

'I know she helped you get away from England after that fiasco with George. And I'm sorry I interfered and sent him here. Mary has told me everything, and I do realise what a mistake I made.'

Touched, Helen hugged her. 'You did what you thought was best. Now, get back to those grandchildren before they tear the place to bits!'

It was therefore much later than she had hoped before she reached the airport and bought a ticket on the next flight to London.

As she had guessed, the plane had plenty of room and she was able to sit by the window, gazing a little wistfully down at the Spanish landscape as they took off. There was so much to see, and she had seen so little! Then before long the pilot announced that they were crossing the Pyrenees into France. Spain was gone, and Helen began to think of what was waiting for her in England.

She would have to get a job as soon as possible. Her parents would welcome her home and tell her she could stay as long as she liked, but they could not afford to support her and she would not let them try to do so. For a few seconds she actually found herself regretting the teacher-training course and the secure job it would have led to, but she had burned her boats as far as that was concerned. Well, she was now an experienced cook and cleaner and not too proud to make use of those skills!

Her spirits sank as they approached the Channel when the pilot came on air again to tell them that it was raining steadily in London. Her suitcase was almost the last off the carousel once they had landed and she walked out past Customs regretting that she could not be extravagant and take a taxi but would have to find her way across London to her friend's flat by Underground.

There was just one man left waiting to meet the plane from Barcelona and when Helen saw him she stared in disbelief. It was John Bridges. He was standing by the passenger exit, dressed in a rather rumpled suit, looking grimly patient. When he saw Helen he took a step forward, then waited as she approached him.

'Welcome home,' he said, taking her case from her.

'What are you doing here?' she asked.

'Waiting for you.'

'How did you know I was coming?'

'Mary emailed a message via Harry Lyne.'

Her mind was a jumble of questions. 'But I didn't know myself which flight I was going to catch until I got to Barcelona.'

'I know,' he said bitterly. 'Mary just said you would be coming back today, so I've had to meet all the flights from Barcelona.'

Helen's eyes widened. 'How long have you been here?'

'Since nine o'clock this morning.'

'Suppose I hadn't been on that plane?'

'Then I would have waited till you did come.'

Suddenly, to his obvious horror, her eyes filled with tears. 'What's the matter?'

Helen sniffed, fumbling for her handkerchief.

'I'm just glad to see you.'

He glanced round desperately, and

then his face lit up. 'Would you like some coffee?'

She nodded and let him lead the way to a coffee shop and waited at a table until he came back with two large cups. For a minute or so they drank coffee while John asked her about Mary and Harry and the children, but she grew impatient with this small talk.

'John, you haven't waited all day to find out how Peter and Shula have been getting on. The last time I saw you, you asked me to dinner and then vanished before I could say anything. Explain why Mary told you I was coming and why you are waiting here.'

He grimaced. 'The last time I saw you, you were in the arms of a golden-haired former boyfriend who was swearing he loved you. There didn't seem any point in hanging about.'

'Oh, you mean George. Well, if you had waited you would have known that I got rid of him very quickly and for good.'

'I didn't know that until I got the

email from Mary and Harry. Apparently they thought I might be interested.'

'Were you?'

John gazed around desperately, and then picked up their empty cups.

'Would you like some more coffee?'

'No,' she said flatly.

'Neither do I,' he sighed, putting the cups down again. 'It's not very good coffee and I've had a lot of it today. In my opinion, there are far too many flights from Barcelona to London.'

Helen lost her patience and thumped the table with a clenched fist, making the cups rattle.

'John Bridges, stop avoiding my questions. I'm tired and I've got to spend the next few days sorting my life out because I haven't got a job and I haven't got anywhere to live. Now I've come back from Spain and found you waiting here, apparently because of some email from my interfering friends, and you won't say why. Tell me the reason instantly or I'm going to walk out of this terminal and you will never see me again!'

John looked at her wryly. 'I'm being an idiot, I know. I am taking as long as possible to tell you because I'm afraid that when I do you will walk out on me.' He gestured at the plastic-topped tables with weary travellers slumped on the uncomfortable little chairs while a bored waitress collected dirty crockery. 'I've imagined having this conversation many times since I got that email. But I always visualised it taking place in some comfortable restaurant, tucked away in a snug little booth which would give us privacy to talk, not in a place like this.'

Helen leant down as if to pick up her bag and he hastily moved it out of her reach.

'Helen, I like you. In fact I like you a lot and after Barcelona I was starting to hope that you liked me as well.' He shook his head. 'I'm avoiding the truth again. I don't just like you, I think I'm falling in love with you. But I thought I loved Michelle, as you thought you loved George, and I don't want just to make any more mistakes. Spain and Barcelona were marvellous, but now we are coming back to real, everyday life, to routine and work. I want us to get to know each other properly. I want to see you again, often. I want to find out if you can love me.'

'In other words,' Helen said softly, 'you want to court me.'

He thought about it. 'Yes.'

Helen was conscious of a bubble of pure happiness swelling inside her.

'Spain was a fairytale. I was the poor cleaning woman and you were the rich man who whisked me off to magnificent hotel, followed by the excitement of being captured by thieves and managing to escape. But, as you say, for a long-term relationship we need to know more about each other. Has either of us got annoying little habits that would drive the other one mad? Can we agree to disagree if we have different opinions on important subjects? Do you prefer white bread or brown bread?'

She leant forward. 'You are a businessman, so let us be business like. I will let you court me, John Bridges, on the condition that if either of us decides we are not suited we will part as friends, with no recriminations or reproaches.'

He gave a sigh of relief. 'That's settled, then! Now, let's get out of this place. Where do you want to go? Mary said you've given up the idea of being a teacher.'

'I am going to stay in London with a friend for a couple of days while I see if I can find work. I have decided I want to write children's stories, so I'll have to find a day job to give me some income.' She smiled mischievously. 'Perhaps I can get a job as a waitress in some comfortable restaurant where you take your business friends for lunch.'

He picked up her bag. 'Do that, and I'll be sure to leave you a big tip.' A thought obviously struck him. 'About money, Helen. I've been poor, now I'm rich, but I could be poor again. I enjoy the luxuries that money can buy but I can live without them. What I am trying to say is that the money itself is not all-important. I enjoy the process of getting it more than the figures on my bank balance.'

'Good. I don't want a man who thinks that money is all that matters. You can enjoy it while you have it. If you do lose it, I'll treat you to a pizza when I can.'

Outside the terminal, he helped her to the car park and up to a very sleek limousine where he put Helen's bag in the boot while she stared at the car.

'What's the matter?' John asked anxiously.

'Somehow, after seeing you wandering round Sitges in jeans and T-shirts, I didn't imagine you driving a car like this.'

He eyed the limousine critically. 'I suppose it is a little ostentatious, but in fact it is a very practical way of getting about London and it is comfortable on long trips. You'll get used to it. I told you I enjoyed some of the things money can buy. This one of them. Now, where does your friend live?'

Helen gave him her friend's address, got in and relaxed against the leather upholstery, and then began to laugh. John looked at her enquiringly but she shook her head. She would explain later. She had dreaded coming home to grim and uncertain life. Now a man who said he loved her, and whom she suspected she loved in return was chauffeuring her across London in a very expensive car.

Whether she and John would be together for always, or whether they would at some time part amicably, the future was definitely going to be fun.